SYMPTOMATIC

An Apocalyptic-Horror Thriller

M.L. Banner

Toes in the Water Publishing, LLC

PRELUDE

When the Rage Began

Before the earth-rattling crash, twelve year-old Dominic Sanchez cast his fishing line into the bay. Almost immediately he got a nibble.

His audience was two of the multitude of stray cats which populated his island. Each meowed its anticipation at what it knew would be coming soon.

"Hey Pedro," he said to the scrawniest of the pair, "hang on. Let me reel 'em in first."

Little Pedro continued his pleading, rubbing up against Dominic's leg for added measure, to remind Dominic that they were waiting to be fed. The larger of the two cats, Beatriz, sat patiently, knowing that Pedro would do the begging for both of them.

Dominic yanked on the rod ever so slightly, snagging the hook deeper into his prey. When he knew he had it, he reeled in the fish. From the line's light drag, he suspected it wasn't very big. And barely a minute later, he pulled the little thing out above the water, where it flopped spasmodically.

"Good news, Pedro. You and your wife eat first. This one's too small for me."

Pedro and his mate both mewed in anxious anticipation.

The palm-sized Corvina was expertly unhooked and tossed to his two furry friends, whirring behind him. The fish bounced once on the wood dock, before Pedro and Beatriz pounced on it. Each immediately snagged a piece from the fish, before nearly a dozen other cats dashed onto the dock to join in the feeding frenzy.

"Hey fellas," Dominic yelled at the approaching clutter, scooting away the biggest of the bunch, already attempting to not only take the remaining Corvina, but the pieces his buddies had pulled from it. "Don't be greedy. Pedro and Beatriz have first dibs on the little fish. And then I get the next one."

Pedro and Beatriz held tight to their tidbits of food and bolted away from the now lifeless carcass, and the swarms of fur around it.

Dominic re-baited his line, getting ready to cast once more. He figured this time, he'd set it out much farther, where the larger schools of fish should be. Hyper-extending his arm over the frantic felines battling for the bony remnants, he shot his friends a quick glance before relaunching.

Pedro ignored the world, already preening himself after inhaling his small but satisfying first meal of the day. Beatriz seemed riveted elsewhere, probably longing for what was coming next.

This time, Dominic put his whole body into his cast, sending his line perfectly into the air.

He snapped his head forward in the direction his lure should land, then immediately convulsed; his shoulders stiffened, his mouth slacked open.

The weighted hook bulleted through the air, targeting its mark perfectly. But on its downward arc, it bounced off the steel hull of a giant fuel barge headed straight for him.

He was so stunned, he let go of his pole and it too sailed outward, plopping a meter or so away into the small bay.

The cats and he scattered down the deck, sure the barge would hit them at any second.

The moment he had turned to run, his ears were assaulted with a grinding noise of metal against sand, and then rocks. Halfway down the wood dock, he was buffeted sideways, and his ears were pummeled by the sounds of boards splintering into thousands of pieces.

Dominic did his best not to trip and fall, while the longer-than-he-ever-remembered dock twisted below him even more.

When he reached the point where the dock's twisted wood met the concrete breaker, the torturous noises had already subsided. He turned to see how far away it was, instantly relieved. The black barge had halted midway through the partially destroyed dock. His breathing became erratic with worry, as he scanned for a sign that they were okay. Then behind the sea wall, a calico tail tentatively approached, telling him his friends were fine.

After a long minute, when there was barely a rattle or squeak from the incoming tide's pushing the stationary ship against the mangled dock, Dominic began to wonder why there was no activity on the deck of the barge. He'd seen this very craft come into the town's small port a few times. The moment its mooring lines were accepted, the small crew would buzz around topside like ants at a picnic. Dominic studied these things because he was going to be a captain of a ship when he grew up.

He glared at the dead ship before him and was surprised that still no one appeared to come topside to see where they had crashed. *Where are they? They couldn't be asleep, could they?*

Dominic spun around to see if anyone else had heard the crash, still not sure what he should do next.

He was all alone.

The creaking and rattling from the ship's hull rubbing against the dock almost felt like it was offering him an invitation to come on board. He had never been on board such a large ship.

Not being one of those boys who only read about things in books, Dominic started back down the dock. But because of the crash, the wood dock had been pushed up in an incline and now led all the way to the deck of the awaiting dead ship at the other end.

Dominic's skin tingled at the thought that maybe everyone onboard could be dead for some reason. *Perhaps the captain had died of a heart attack: old people were always dying of heart attacks.* The cool breeze taunted his crawling skin further. His imagination produced an image of what the captain's dead body might look like, draped over the pegs of the ship's steering wheel.

An upturned board and his lack of attention caused Dominic to stumble.

It didn't slow him down. Dominic leaned into his ascension and mounted the dock's steepest incline, which appeared to lead directly to the ship's edge. It looked like he could literally walk right onto the ship's forecastle, which was his plan.

Without even looking at it, he passed by the familiar stenciling on the ship's side, announcing, "Ramirez Fuel Services SA, Punta Delgado, Spain."

Once at the newly created dock-edge, now bunched up and ragged, he hopped over the two inch span and landed on top of the deck. He froze and listened for someone to tell him to leave. Anyone.

He'd never been on top of a fuel barge, not really having any interest in this type of ship: he wanted to captain a cruise ship or a large luxury yacht. His only boating experience so far was rowing a neighbor's small row boat.

Other than the ship rubbing against the broken mess of what was left of their dock and a stiff breeze whistling its own tune, all Dominic heard was Pedro's purring right below him. *This ship is a ghost town.*

He shuddered at this thought.

His gaze drifted down to his buddy, about to ask if he was ready to explore the ship, when he noticed he was standing in a large puddle of red, starkly cast against the ship's white decking.

It was blood. Lots of blood.

Vila de Corvo's PCP Police Chief, Salvadore Calderon, slammed the door of his Skoda. Almost immediately he blew out an exaggerated whistle at the sight before them. "Well Tomas, here's one more thing you wouldn't see on the mainland."

Tomas Novo, the youngest of his two agents, who had pleaded with him to be released into a larger, more exciting police unit on the Portuguese mainland, said nothing. The young man adjusted his hat and waited for his superior. When Sal took up a place beside him, he too gawked at the wrecked hundred-year-old dock and the ship that caused the damage, wedged into the middle of it. Tomas asked, "Do you think she'll leak?"

"I'm more worried about why I don't see any of the crew, and what caused the crash," Sal said. His voice scattered into the wind as he stomped onto the dock. It felt as if it was moving with the tide.

Sal considered his own questions, and then wondered if this day could get any stranger. He and his agent had just returned from investigating two separate animal attacks and then a report of some crazy woman killing her husband. Now this. Their small station was barely two kilometers away. So when they heard the crash, it seemed like the whole town had poured outside of their homes and shops to see what all the clatter was about.

"Tomas, get on your radio and have Val call Ramirez Shipping in Puento Delgado. See if they know their ship has crashed onto our shore.

His junior agent started hollering inaudibly into his radio, while Sal mounted the inclined dock, which ended at the starboard bow of the ship.

Sal tried to block out Tomas' voice to listen for any other sounds. Other than the wind and the creaking of ship against the broken dock, he heard nothing.

When Sal hopped onto the barge's deck, he immediately knew something was very wrong, and drew his service Berretta in response.

Tomas hollered something else into the radio and froze beside him upon seeing his superior's drawn weapon.

Sal pointed, without saying anything. A puddle of blood and the bloody sneaker prints of a child led toward the open doorway a few meters ahead.

When they heard a little boy's scream, they both went running.

They followed the bloody trail, but with each of their footfalls, Sal felt his anxiety spike. Twice he glanced back at Tomas to confirm it wasn't some hallucination. He felt like he was seeing things lately, so maybe he was imagining some of this. Each time Tomas met his gaze with the same "this is some crazy shit" look, he knew it was real. He wanted to say to him each time, "Well you wanted some excitement... here it is." But he held off saying anything until they finished running the insanely long distance from the bow to the doorway.

It was an entrance into the bowels of the ship, where the blood-trail stopped. The door swayed slightly from the ship's rocking motion, forced upon it by the incoming tide.

Sal was a little out of breath and was relieved when looking back, that his young agent was as well.

"It sounded like a male child to me," Tomas stated, obviously trying to smooth out his own growing anxiousness.

He was right, it was a young boy, and the shriek sounded familiar to him as well. He probably knew this kid, because he knew everyone in their town. "Follow me," he said and then glared at his deputy. "Don't shoot unless you have to." He didn't want to get shot in the back by the nervous young man.

Tomas nodded, holding his service weapon down with both hands.

The entrance led into a dark stairwell, which almost immediately descended into a dank murk. A blinking light below flashed a momentary view of the emptiness.

An animal screeched a hollow bray, like it was injured and angry.

It was close.

Sal had a sinking dread that this might be another animal attack, although he had no reason to connect the two attacks on his island with this crash. His heart began pumping ample amounts of adrenaline to his systems. Something else seemed wrong.

Was it him?

In all of his years in police work, he remained safe by being careful to avoid risky situations. Only when one of his men was in peril did he put himself into peril and then, only after he waited for the last possible moment. He felt different now. He felt like he didn't care, even if it was risky. Worse, he was looking forward to whatever was down there. His heart pumped happily; his chest heaved joyfully. He should have been terrified, just like his agent was.

Then he heard another bray, much closer now. A form appeared in the yellowish light of the flashing strobe. It wasn't an animal. It was a man. It was Old Man Ramirez, the captain and owner of this ship. Ramirez lifted his gaze up the stairwell to meet Sal's and screeched at him. Sal knew then that Ramirez was making the animal sounds he had heard, like he was the animal. Ramirez' eyes blazed red like two turn signals with each flash of light; they appeared to blink at him. Ramirez then turned and disappeared.

Sal didn't hesitate. He stepped into the darkness.

Part III

SYMPTOMATIC

"Your eye is the lamp of your body.
When your eyes are good, your whole body also is full of
light.
But when they are bad, your body also is full of darkness."
Holy Bible, NIV, Luke 11:34

01

The Vote (Eleven Days Later)

"I t's their blooming eyes," Boris bellowed. His face twisted into a frown, which Chloe Barton couldn't see in the darkness. "Their damned red eyes. That's how you know they're animals."

"But they're not animals, they're still people..." Chloe pleaded. "They're infected with a disease and they're just not in control of what they do."

"Suppose you'd say the same thing about pedophiles: it's not their fault, they don't know what they do. So what? Should we feel sorry for them because they're diseased?" This came from an officer on the other side of the group. She didn't know him.

Chloe sighed, feeling like she was swimming against the current in a river of piranhas. "I'm not saying that. I'm just saying that killing them all isn't the answer. And it's not who we are as people."

Boris burst out of his aluminum chair, almost knocking it down. "Hon, I'm saying that's exactly what we are. The sooner we kill all of the parasitics, the better. For all of us."

"Shhhh. Someone's coming," one of their group huffed.

Every one of their group held their breaths. All heads turned to see who it was. A single set of footsteps, barely heard over the stiff sea breeze, grew louder with each footfall. Someone was definitely coming their way.

Chloe shrank back into the group, not really wanting to be seen by anyone, especially another officer. As the head of the ship's medical clinic, it didn't feel right to be at a Resist Parasitics meeting. She glanced at the faces, most cloaked in shadows. She knew many of them; it was hard not to, with so few of the original crew left. Some she didn't know, because they either worked in areas she'd just never visited, or they were originally passengers, like Boris.

She was amazed by people like Boris, who she understood to be infected with the parasite which had turned many men into monsters. He just hadn't become symptomatic yet. But he could at any time. Then what would he do, order his own death? Highly doubtful. It was just his fear talking.

They were all fearful, especially of what lay ahead of them. It seemed like they had some control of things, but this control felt tenuous at best. So everyone wanted safety and they were willing to sacrifice anything to get it, including every sense of morality they had. Well, she wasn't going to be a part of this. She didn't have an answer yet for their parasitics, but she wasn't going to stand for genocidal murder. It just wasn't right.

The footsteps were almost upon them, now echoing off the pool decking.

A few of the craned necks retracted back from the edge of the outdoor movie theater screen, seemingly satisfied with the footsteps' owner.

"It's just Bohdan. He's one of us," said someone she couldn't see.

Bohdan Oliynyk was a despicable man, of the lowest order. A Czech from engineering, he'd been in two days ago, complaining of a sore throat. When Chloe said that she was in charge of this medical center, he refused to leave until a male doctor would see him, saying that he never trusted the words of a woman who wasn't even a doctor.

Luckily for Chloe, a male nurse, who was a passenger volunteer, saw him, diagnosed him as having acute pharyngitis, and gave him some antibiotics and sent him away.

She had hoped he would have remained sealed in engineering. She shrank further into the darkness.

"Good timing, Bohdan." Paulo from security and the organizer of this meeting spoke up. "We'd just been discussing whether or not we should treat the crazies like good, misunderstood people or just kill them. We were close to voting. Do you want—"

"Let's vote. No more discussions," Bohdan stated.

"Okay, all who want to do nothing about the crazies, locked away in our lounge, where one day they may break out and eat us all, say 'Aye.'"

Only one other person, a meek-sounding man, said "Aye" along with Chloe.

"All those who want to terminate the abominations before they kill us all, say 'Nay.'"

A resounding "Nay" sounded from the group.

"The Nays have it. Now, let's discuss how we should do this."

Chloe stood up from her chair and couldn't disappear from this place quickly enough. As she stepped away, trying to hug the shadows, she heard Bohdan speak up.

"I have a way to do this and I can do it tomorrow morning."

02

Ted

S he stood over him while he slept. His cabin was void of light, and yet she watched and listened to him mumble something from an ongoing nightmare.

She slithered out of her long sleeve athletic jersey and then her shorts. Pulling the covers back, she slid into his bed, inching her way toward him. Her hand found him, knowing what he liked.

After a few seconds, he moaned softy. She smiled at this.

She guided herself on top of him and moved her hips slowly. His moans grew in response and he began to move with her.

"You're all mine now," she whispered.

His eyes popped open and he glared at her. Her grin was Grand Canyon-sized, and equally rapturous. He knew her contagious smile all too well. But this one was different. It felt wrong.

He didn't know why, until it became obvious.

It was pitch-black in the cabin and yet the features of her face and body were absolutely clear. She looked perfect: equal portions of delicately strong and delightfully sexy.

She grinned even more at his revelation, if that was possible. She moved her hips faster, and he saw that he was matching her motions. They were one. Even her eyes—both ruby-red now—pulsed in perfect synchronicity to their movements and their heartbeats. His breathing grew more rapid, as did hers, as if he were breathing for her.

Or is she breathing for me?

The logical side of his brain was stuck on figuring out how he could see her in the darkness. He couldn't resolve this, even if he accepted everything else. And yet her ghostly outline was as clear as if there were a full moon somehow casting its eerie glow on her. Some of her details even seemed as clear as they would be during a midday sun.

But how?

"You're wondering how you can see me," she stated, as if she could read his thoughts too.

He froze.

The chasm-sized smile slid off her face. "Don't stop dear, we're just getting started."

He could feel his mouth fall open, now gaping.

She leaned over him, pressing her bare chest against his, and softly took in his lips with hers. She kissed him passionately, but then abruptly pulled back. "You're one of us now."

She drifted farther back from him, but her legs and thighs remained clasped around him. Her hands still clutched his hips, and then locked into him even tighter. She wanted him to know that she had total control over him and his movements.

She was so strong now, so much stronger than he thought she could be. And he knew that she could crush him, snap him in two if she wanted to. But she didn't; she just wanted him to know that she had that kind of power over him.

He accepted it.

She released one hand from his hip. It slowly rose in the air above him, as if floating, her fist and forefinger becoming a pointer. She was guiding his glare to the other side of the bed, to what was supposed to be her side.

He turned his head in that direction, anxious to find out what she was trying to tell him. Gone was the shock that he could clearly see his cabin in total darkness, because he knew what she said was right. He had somehow become like her now, and this terrified him.

Even though each of her features and many of his cabin's details were crystal clear, he couldn't quite make out the moving form beside him. Blinking away at the darkness, he couldn't tell what it was, only that there was something under the covers, on her side of the bed. Then based on its size and shape, he knew it wasn't a something; it was a someone. They weren't alone now.

Repelled by this, he tried to move away from the writhing mass, which he could now see more clearly and even hear its rustle. But she held him down, still controlling him, demanding he see this. He gave up.

"Open your eyes, dear," she commanded, her voice sultry but serious.

It was then he realized his eyes had been closed. He didn't want to see who or what was in the bed with them. And whatever it was now rustled even more. And it groaned.

He flicked open his eyes, piercing the darkness once more. And he saw the form was out from under the sheets, sitting up in their bed.

Recognition slapped him in the face.

It was Jean Pierre, their acting captain. The same man she had been working with earlier on an FBI investigation, just before she had changed. Jean Pierre was here, in their bed.

If that wasn't enough of a shock to his system, he realized that something was terribly wrong with this man.

Jean Pierre was gasping for breath. Gagging. At the same time, his hands were clasped around his neck. Thick streams of blood seeped through the gaps in his fingers. A dark red liquid coursed down his formal clothes and pooled all around him.

His face was a surreal death mask of terror. He tried to cry out for help, but it came out as a slight whimper. "Hellllpa."

"Oh my God, what did you do?" Ted barked as his eyes drilled into hers.

She bellowed back in laughter. "You did this, Ted. You're a killer now, just like me."

He coughed, because his mouth was full of something soft... chewy. He spat it out; a fleshy mess plopped into a puddle pooled beside him. The pool was blood... Jean Pierre's blood. And its sticky warmth coated his mouth, his body and now... hers.

At that very moment Ted was both excitedly aroused and utterly terrified. "Nooooo!"

She cackled in response, until her laughter fractured and faded into an almost scratchy-sounding voice that demanded, "Ted, are you there?"

Her voice became more distant, almost disconnected from her, like she was a ventriloquist throwing her words out into murk, where they became consumed by the night.

Once again, a scratchy call to him from the other side of the room, only louder this time, "Ted, are you there?"

The staticky voice chimed once again, "Ted, are you there?"

He flicked his eyes open and closed, and then open again, because he could no longer see her in the darkness. He couldn't see anything.

His right hand shot out of the covers and he felt along the wall, in a desperate search for the switch.

Clicking it on, blinding white light burst throughout his cabin. He drilled his eyes forward to where his wife had been. She was no longer there. He snapped his head to his left, expecting to see the bloody man—who was it again? He was gone too.

It was Jean Pierre. That's who was there.

It was all just an awful nightmare. Nothing more.

"Ted, are you there?" called the portable radio on his nightstand. "This is Captain Jean Pierre; please answer if you can hear me."

DAY TWELVE

LIKE MOST PEOPLE IN THE WORLD, THIS DAY BEGAN AFTER A NIGHTMARE. FOR ME, THE NIGHTMARE ENDED WHEN I WOKE UP; FOR MOST EVERYONE ELSE, THE NIGHTMARE CONTINUES.

MANY ONBOARD OUR SHIP ARE CAUTIOUSLY HOPEFUL THAT WE'VE PUT OUR NIGHTMARE BEHIND US. MEANWHILE, THE REST OF THE WORLD IS STILL CLOAKED IN UNENDING DEATH AND DESTRUCTION. EVEN IF WE SURVIVE THE COMING DAYS, THE NIGHTMARE WILL STILL BE ALL AROUND US, LIKE THE DARK, FOREBODING CLOUDS NOW BLANKETING ALL THE HEAVENS. WE'RE NOT SURE IF THIS IS NORMAL AZURIAN WEATHER OR A SIGN OF MORE DARKNESS YET TO COME.

STILL THERE IS REASON FOR HOPE.

WHEN THE RAGE HIT US LIKE A TIDAL WAVE, IT APPEARED THAT WE WOULD SUFFER THE SAME FATE AS THE REST OF THE WORLD. I ADMIT TO LOSING HOPE AT TIMES, FIRST WITH SO MANY PASSENGERS AND CREW LOSING THEIR LIVES AND THE REMAINDER TURNING INTO SOME NEW FORM OF MONSTER, ALL SEEMINGLY CONTROLLED BY A SIMPLE PARASITE. THEN WE CONFIRMED THIS WAS HAPPENING EVERYWHERE.

FROM ONGOING NEWS REPORTS, UNTIL WE STOPPED RECEIVING THEM, THE SAME TIDAL WAVE OF MADNESS WASHED OVER THE WORLD, LEAVING ALMOST NO ONE UNAFFECTED. BILLIONS OF RAGE-FUELED ANIMALS AND MILLIONS OF BLOOD-THIRSTY HUMANS ATTACKED ANYTHING WITH A HEARTBEAT THAT WAS NOT ALREADY INFECTED. INDEED, THE PROSPECTS FOR ANYONE'S SURVIVAL LOOKED BLEAKER THAN AT ANY TIME IN HUMAN HISTORY.

STILL, AS A SCIENTIST, IT'S HARD NOT TO LOOK WITH AWE AND APPRECIATION AT WHAT MAY BE THE DAWN OF A NEW SPECIES. THESE PARASITICS (THAT'S WHAT WE CALL THOSE WHO ARE FULLY CONTROLLED BY THE RAGE DISEASE) ARE SURE TO BE THE NEW APEX ON EARTH, THE TOP DOG IN THE FOOD CHAIN. AS A LIFE-LONG ATHEIST, I BEGAN TO ACCEPT THE FATE THAT HAD BEEN DEALT US HUMANS: EXTINCTION WAS LIKELY JUST AROUND THE CORNER.

AND YET, I CANNOT DISCOUNT THE THEORY THAT SOME PROVIDENTIAL HAND WAS AT WORK HERE, AS ILLOGICAL AS THAT MAY SOUND.

HOW ELSE DO I REASON THAT MY WIFE AND I ENDED UP ON ONE OF THE FEW SURVIVABLE PLACES TO WEATHER THIS KIND OF APOCALYPSE? BEING ON A CRUISE SHIP AFFORDED US CONTROL OVER OUR ENVIRONMENT, WHICH ALLOWED US TO TILT THE EVOLUTIONARY SCALES BACK TO OUR FAVOR. TALK ABOUT TRUTH BEING STRANGER THAN FICTION. I CERTAINLY COULDN'T HAVE WRITTEN THIS NARRATIVE: AN AUTHOR WHO WROTE A BOOK ON THIS VERY APOCALYPSE AND A PARASITOLOGIST (AN EXPERT AT WHAT'S GOING ON) SERENDIPITOUSLY APPEAR ON THE SAME SHIP, JUST AS THE WAVES OF ATTACKS ON THE MAINLAND WERE STARTING.

BEING ON A SELF-CONTAINED SHIP REMOVED US FROM THE PREDATOR-TO-PREY IMBALANCE ON THE MAINLAND, WITH TEN THOUSAND MAMMALS—MORE THAN THE MAJORITY OF THEM INFECTED—TO EVERY HUMAN. YET BY HAVING JUST A FEW ANIMALS ON BOARD, WE COULD USE

WHAT WE LEARNED FROM THEM TO HELP US SURVIVE THE WAVE OF HUMAN PARASITIC ATTACKS THAT FOLLOWED NEXT. WE FOUND OUT, QUITE BY ACCIDENT, THAT WE COULD CONTROL THE PARASITICS BY LOWERING THEIR BODY TEMPERATURE, AND THIS COULD BE ACCOMPLISHED BY DROPPING THE OUTSIDE TEMPERATURE USING THE SHIP'S AIR CONDITIONING. COULD ALL OF THIS SIMPLY BE FORTUITOUS?

THEN THERE ARE THE UNASSAILABLE TRUTHS CONCERNING MY WIFE, WHICH CANNOT BE EASILY EXPLAINED AS RANDOM CHANCE.

TJ CONTRACTED THE VERY PARASITE AT THE ROOT OF THIS WORLDWIDE APOCALYPSE FROM AN ANIMAL ATTACK YEARS AGO. AND YET IF SHE HADN'T, SHE WOULD HAVE SURELY DIED WHEN SHE FELL FROM THAT ZIP LINE. AND BECAUSE SHE BECAME SYMPTOMATIC, EVERY ONE OF THE SHIP'S SURVIVORS HAS HER AND HER NEW ABILITIES TO THANK, AMONG THE MANY REASONS FOR OUR MAKING IT THIS FAR. IT'S TRUE THAT HER "ABILITIES" DID NOT COME WITHOUT COST—MY HEART STILL BREAKS AT OUR INDEFINITE SEPARATION.

BUT THAT'S A WORRY FOR ANOTHER DAY.

AND AS EXPECTED, WE HAVE ANOTHER CHALLENGE AHEAD OF US, BUT AT THE SAME TIME, A POTENTIAL SOLUTION. FORTUITOUS OR PROVIDENTIAL? I'LL LET YOU BE THE JUDGE.

WHEN HALF THE POPULATION OF OUR SHIP APPEARED TO GO INSANE AND STARTED ATTACKING, TWO OF THE PARASITICS GOT ONTO THE BRIDGE AND DESTROYED SOME OF OUR CONTROLS. IN THE PROCESS, OUR SHIP DUMPED MOST OF ITS FUEL INTO THE OCEAN. WE DIDN'T REALIZE THIS UNTIL AFTER WE HAD TAKEN BACK CONTROL OF THE SHIP.

ONCE AGAIN, THIS WOULD PROBABLY HAVE BEEN OUR END: WE NEEDED THE AIR CONDITIONING TO KEEP THE PARASITICS' BODY TEMPERATURES LOW ENOUGH THAT THEY'D REMAIN IN A SEMI-HYBERNATIVE STATE. AND WE

NEEDED FUEL TO RUN THE AIR CONDITIONERS AND THE REST OF THE SHIP'S SYSTEMS. AND WITH THE WORLD IN CHAOS, INCLUDING ALL OF THE MAJOR PORTS, SAFELY FINDING THE NEEDED FUEL WOULD HAVE BEEN NEARLY IMPOSSIBLE AT BEST. THEN IT WOULD SEEM PROVIDENCE'S HAND OFFERED US A SOLUTION.

AMONG THE LOUD QUIET OF THE WORLD'S NOW EMPTY AIRWAVES, I FOUND A BROADCAST FROM AN ISLAND WHERE THEY SAY RAGE HASN'T HIT AND ITS OCCUPANTS HAVE THE FUEL WE NEED, IN EXCHANGE FOR A LITTLE OF OUR FOOD. SURE, IT SOUNDS TOO GOOD TO BE TRUE. AND PERHAPS IT IS.

ASSUMING THEIR INTENTIONS ARE GENUINE AND WE HAVE WHAT THEY WANT, I SUPPOSE A DEAL SHOULD BE MADE. WHO KNOWS, MAYBE THIS ISLAND WILL END UP BEING OUR NEW HOME.

CERTAINLY WITHOUT THIS ONLY OPTION, WE WILL BE DEAD IN THE WATER IN A FEW HOURS. AND THAT MEANS WE WOULD LOSE ANY CONTROL WE HAD OVER THE PARASITICS. GAME OVER.

THEN THERE'S THE NEWEST CHALLENGE: INDUCTION OF ALL PASSENGERS INTO THE CREW. IT WAS A BOLD MOVE BY OUR CAPTAIN. AND NOW, WE ARE NO LONGER A CRUISE OF LEISURE: WE'VE BECOME A FREIGHTER OF HOPE, FIGHTING FOR A COMMON GOAL, SURVIVAL. NO LONGER WERE THERE TWO CLASSES OF PEOPLE: CREW, WHOSE JOB IT WAS TO SERVE, AND THE PASSENGERS, WHO EXPECTED TO BE SERVED. EVERYONE WAS GIVEN A JOB TO DO, AND EVERYONE WAS EXPECTED TO DO IT, OR THEY WOULD BE DROPPED OFF AT THE NEXT PORT.

ALONG WITH OUR RATIONED FOOD, THIS WAS ALL THE NEW NORMAL. WE ALL WORK MANY HOURS TO HELP ALL ON BOARD SURVIVE UNTIL THE NEXT DAY AND THAT MAKES OUR DAYS PASS BY QUICKLY, LEAVING LITTLE TIME FOR ANY OF US TO WORRY ABOUT WHAT'S GOING ON OUTSIDE THIS SHIP.

WHEN I DO TAKE TIME TO PONDER OUR WORLD, WHICH IS ACTUALLY PART OF MY DUTIES, I CAN'T HELP BUT THINK OF MY WIFE, TJ, AND WHEN I CAN SEE HER AGAIN. IT'S WHAT I LOOK FORWARD TO.

AND TODAY AFTER MY REGULAR MEETING WITH MOLLY, WHO SAYS SHE HAS AN "INCREDIBLE REVELATION" SHE'S DYING TO TELL ME ABOUT, I WILL GET TO SEE TJ BRIEFLY. THEN SHE AND THE OTHERS WILL ATTEMPT TO MAKE A TRADE. I'LL BE HELPING WITH THAT ONE VIA THE RADIO.

BUT THE BEST PART OF THE WHOLE DAY WILL BE SEEING MY WIFE.

I GUESS LIFE HAS COME DOWN TO LOOKING FORWARD TO THOSE SMALL THINGS... SMALL TO SOME, BUT GIANT TO OTHERS.

03

TJ

She awoke with a startled shake. Not from the room's coolness, but shock at finding herself sitting on the edge of her unmade bed, in the dark of this foreign cabin. TJ had been doing a lot of this since her rebirth: finding herself in places she didn't remember getting to.

She glanced down at her Orion necklace, currently lacking all luster. *There was no light in the cabin to reflect,* she told herself. But it was still clear enough, as if illuminated by bright moonlight. She had it cupped in her open hands, watching it move up and down with the rapid heaving of her chest.

She pressed her palms, and with it her necklace, back onto her breasts and allowed her eyes to shut, in a desperate attempt to recall the wonderful dream she had just had of Ted, before the evil within her invaded this rare respite with her husband and forced her awake.

The features of his face came to mind...

He no longer had a mustache!

She smiled at this.

Then she remembered the blood.

Her eyes flicked open and she pushed away the images. Looking down again, she shuddered, at once realizing she was squeezing much too hard upon the delicate gift commemorating their 20th wedding anniversary, given to her only a few long days ago. She was terrified she would smash one of the last tangible connections she had between her, her husband and her old life. But there were far more terrifying things than this.

Pulling at the elastic of her compression shorts, she slipped the necklace inside, feeling comfort in it resting against her skin—since the chain broke, it was the only way she could keep it secured to her. She shot up from the bed, her feet once again finding the path she was sure she was wearing into the carpet by now.

The pacing up and down the length of the cabin was one of the few actions she felt in control of; it was her way to physically force back the mental tides raging within her, all of which desired to burst out and consume what little remained of her old human self.

Her mind was an ongoing battlefield where a war was being fought between the armies of good thoughts or memories and evil aspirations or desires. Whichever side won would claim her soul.

At times, she was able to recall the delicate trickle of the lovely memories of Ted, her family, their home, and even her work. It was only during those times that she could actually find some peace and with it, sleep. But sleep, like the comforts of her old memories, was fleeting and brief.

During the remaining moments—the majority of the time—her thoughts were a windswept mental seascape of sin, a tempest of anger, a downpour of hatred, a hurricane of murderous rage, a destructive desire for blood. And when these thoughts were allowed into her mind, she felt like she was set on an unstoppable course to kill, or to maim, or to at least hurt whoever got in her way. It was during those times, times like now, that she would find herself wide awake. Hyperventilating. Although she was always breathing as if she were hyperventilating. One of the many things that had changed in her.

And it was all the changes that had manifested themselves inside her, and were still occurring, that led her to separate herself from Ted. He didn't understand. But how could he? She didn't really understand—was trying to understand—what was going on inside her brain and body.

She had told him that she had to remain separate, because she didn't feel he would be safe around her. And this was partially true, because she was afraid that her terrifying desire for human flesh would be unstoppable in close quarters. And when either passion or anger sprang forth, it brought with it an overwhelming sensation, even an unquenchable thirst, for murder and blood. And these desires could arise with the simple whiff of her next meal, all because of her new ability to smell everything...

Like some goddamn dog... Scratch that, like some damned hound from hell.

Great, just like me to develop a dog ability.

Most things simply smelled bad, like the body odor of another infected. But a non-infected's smell was frighteningly the complete opposite. Because of this, she worried that even the mere aroma of the uninfected could set her off. And it was why she wore a swimming nose-plug: to stem the smells of those who were not infected, like her husband.

But weren't these all just excuses?

After all, a part of her—an ever-shrinking part of her—that was still human and still loved him and badly needed him didn't really believe she would allow that evil part of her to take total control and hurt him. Although she reasoned thus, with each internal battle between good and evil, and with each noticeable physical change, she was a little less sure of this.

The largest part of her worry of their being together was that he would see the changes in her. And not just the physical.

It was her internal battles that she wanted the most to hide from him. She feared—one of the few fears she possessed anymore—that he could see some horrendous evil inside of her. She couldn't stand to see him repulsed by her becoming some sort of monster. That's really what kept her away. So she told herself, and him, that this separation would only last until she could figure this thing out. And get control of it.

This made sense to both of them, since she always had control of things. Even when she was deathly afraid of animals, she remained in control by staying out of situations where fear would rear its ugly head. In this way, she didn't allow fear to control her. Amongst all of the new changes in her, she'd lost her fear of animals, along with all the other normal human fears. Ironically, the less fear she felt, the more she felt like she was losing control.

Something outside of her consciousness was fighting for possession of her mind and body, tempting her with euphoric tastes and desires, and alluring her with fantastic abilities. But she would continue to fight for her humanity, even though she didn't know what it was going to do with her next. She wasn't going to let it win. Whatever it was.

"Yeah, I know what you are," she stated out loud so it could hear her. As if it worked that way.

She guessed that she must have been originally infected with this parasite when she was viciously attacked by that crazed dog. Ted said the dog's saliva could have introduced the parasite into her bloodstream. He had also said that this parasite had been around for centuries; it just wasn't as widespread until recently. And when the thermo-bacilli were spewed into the atmosphere, that's what ignited this whole apocalypse upon them.

She once more was surprised to find herself stopped, mid-step from her pacing, standing before the cabin's full-length mirror. There, she examined herself.

TJ found comfort in the darkness during moments like this, even though in this mirror, she could see the details of her own face and body. The colors were all different without light. She wasn't sure if there were any colors in the darkness, with her mind filling in the colors, albeit poorly.

Once again, she marveled at the physical changes which had occurred, as she focused on her chest rising and falling.

She had to admit that she was thrilled to have gained the ability to see not only long distances, but in the dark as well. Her whole life—at least for as long as she could remember—she was plagued with grotesque nearsightedness, barely able to see past her own two feet. She always wore glasses, giving her a bookish look during puberty. Later in life she found the freedom of contacts, and that's when the boys started to notice her more. Later still, as she got older, she could see a little better at a distance, while at the same time losing her ability to see things close. But all that changed with her rebirth. But with her new sight abilities came her creepy red eyes. Or at least one red eye.

She leaned over to the light switch, flipped it on and completely blinded herself.

After shaking away ghostly white flashes, she resumed her place in front of the mirror, where she examined her eyes again. She had to force herself not to squint against the cabin's bright lights.

Both Dr. Molly Simmons and Ted had explained that it had something to do with the loss of melanin. Gone were her blue eyes. One now was a pinkish-blue and the other a bright crimson—like blood. The same hue as those of her symptomatic brothers and sisters who seemed to have turned crazy after their own rebirths. They told her that the loss of melanin drained her of her color. But it wasn't just her eyes; it was her skin too.

In the stark lighting of this cabin, she now looked like death warmed over. And with each day, her skin lost more of its life. She was becoming some sort of albino. Although never dark-skinned—far from it—she at least had had a little pigment, especially in contrast to her blonde hair. She had even hoped to add to her skin's color on this cruise, by spending time in the warmth of the sun.

But I can at least do something about my outward appearance.

She shed her clothes and stepped into the cool spray of the shower—the lever at its coldest setting—and she washed away the grime that clung to her, more naturally than before.

After drying off, she slid on a fresh set of exercise clothes, her normal uniform now. The material breathed, allowing her to stay cool, which was of the utmost importance now. And because it was so form-fitting, she felt she had a free range of motion, which also felt important if she had to use her new abilities.

After pulling her hair into a tight ponytail, she grabbed the bottle of self-tanning lotion from the counter. She procured this from the same place she'd found the swimmer's nose plugs: the ship's gift shop. After shaking it up, she squeezed a healthy portion onto a palm and then smoothed it into one arm and then the other.

Not bad, she thought after examining her work.

She applied lotion up her shoulders, around the exposed skin of her chest, and then felt skilled enough at this to apply some to her blanched face.

She scrutinized herself in the bathroom mirror.

This might actually work.

After making sure she was well covered, she applied just a little makeup, finding a rosier color of lipstick than she would have normally worn: like the rest of her skin, her lips needed all the help they could get.

Finally she stepped back and analyzed herself against a mental picture of what was previously "normal," turning and tilting her head at different angles for confirmation. She felt like she was ready.

04

Molly

D r. Molly Simmons removed her glasses and attempted to rub away the fatigue nested in her eyes. Last she looked, her scleras were as red as the irises of her parasitic subjects. It was no use. She was done.

She gave up holding herself erect, now allowing her body to tilt backwards in the reclining chair the captain had given her. This gift was so she could do her work better. "Work? Ha!" she chided herself.

I'm supposed to be a retired parasitologist. Key word is retired.

With her eyes closed, and her back finally supported for the first time in hours, Molly considered what led to these late hours of work on a former luxury cruise ship.

Before retirement, when she had been working regular hours—another oxymoronic concept for a scientist at any age—all she did was research, usually for corporate laboratories, whose sole interest was in finding the next big cure for the various parasitic illnesses. After she retired, she wrote a few papers on some of the potential coming crises that could come from some of the bigger parasitic challenges, including the subject of her current research, Toxoplasmosis. It was her futurist predictions that garnered her some of her notoriety.

With this notoriety came offers to speak, but she rarely accepted them. After all, she was retired. She did accept a couple of offers so she could also to visit her daughter in Northern Florida. Most recently it was the opportunity see her granddaughter in France, whom she hadn't seen since before she was married. So she traveled across the Atlantic to give a speech to a bunch of stodgy old men—there were few women in her field in Europe. And that was the extent of her "work," at least before this cruise.

When she had worked, there were few pressures other than those of self-imposed deadlines. She had loved every moment of what she did, even the long hours in her lab. She hated her work now.

The self-imposed pressures to find answers for her captain, her new author-friend Ted Williams and all the people on her ship were almost debilitating.

She breathed out a long groan, an equal mixture of frustration at being in this position and the extreme exhaustion she was feeling. The lack of sleep was at the root of all of this.

She'd slept little on this ship. How could she, as she was spending every waking moment reacting to one colossal problem after another? That was the nub of it. Proper research was never done during a crisis. It should be conducted in the vacuum of discovery, with lots of time. No matter the problem, she knew she could discover an answer, if given enough time. And it was often the motivation that drove her. That and a good laboratory.

She snickered at this, since her laboratory now was a videotape room and a couple of video cameras trained on her subjects.

Molly let her mind wander as she felt the weight of her eyelids, relishing these rare moments of peace and self-reflection... *And no back pain,* she thought.

It must have been the angle in which she was resting in this chair, and the pillows she had jammed around it. Her disease-riddled back often screamed at her to change position every few minutes. Rarely could she consciously remember not feeling that screaming pain. Not even in the soft beds the ship provided. She could almost fall asleep here. But her mind was racing too much.

So she took this opportunity to reflect on something delightful: her travel abroad and seeing her granddaughter's new family. *Hard to believe that it had all started three weeks ago. It felt longer.*

Molly's granddaughter Lola and her French husband Claude had encouraged her to accept the speaking engagement and go on this cruise. That's exactly what Molly did, first spending time with Lola and Claude on his family's winery in the Loire region of France.

She caught her breath when her mind wondered about their current fate. She now illogically reasoned that they'd be safe there; that they'd be left untouched by this apocalypse. She couldn't bear to think otherwise.

After her visit, Molly was the guest of the Universitat de Barcelona, Spain, speaking to some of the world's leading parasitologists at an annual conference. She had warned them all about a pending crisis, saying that all the signs were there, with increased animal attacks, along with widespread paranoia and schizophrenic behavior in humans. She shook her head at how right she was about that.

After this, she headed to Malaga to board the cruise ship, with the single goal of relaxing while sailing across the Atlantic. She had brought a couple of books to read, but mostly she would enjoy the pleasure of being waited on by someone who wasn't one of her family members. The whole trip would have culminated with Molly meeting up with her daughter in Florida.

But then the world fell apart.

She sprang forward in her chair, sling-shotting her spiking anger toward her desk, so she could address the perpetrator of this apocalypse. She stared down at her desktop; a printout of the giant-sized protozoa gazed back. "It's all because of you!" She punched the color-enhanced photograph, a close-up of a toxoplasma gondii parasite. "You're the cause of this whole mess." Her forefinger sliced down on the parasite's picture, as if it were that easy to do harm to this microscopic monster.

Her anger quickly subsided, and so did the rest of her energy. With this and her quick movements, the chronic pain in her back had returned in full force. She tried again to alleviate this, by falling back again into her chair and the comfort it provided. There was a reason why she had retired: she was too damned old for these late-night research events. *But there was no use in complaining about this, was there?* she again chided herself.

This time, she sat up more gingerly and leaned into her desk, organizing the papers which currently littered its top.

The recent online research papers Mr. Buzz had found for her on university databases had proven invaluable to her research. He was somehow able to rig up a way to connect up to their servers even though he said most of the Internet was down. She didn't exactly understand how it all worked, only that Mr. Buzz said he used some sort of mesh network connection to search and find digitized texts, studies, and other useful information, based on some select keywords Molly had given him. All of which he had printed for her.

She had just read through a majority of the recent batch. With these, she was able to compare the most current T-Gondii research studies with what she and Mr. Deep had observed. She sat up straighter in her seat, now looking at her pages of notes chronicling what they now knew based on their own empirical observations.

So much had changed with what they'd learned over the six days of their observing the parasitics they had locked up in the ship's largest lounge.

At first, they seemed no more than wild animals, uniquely focused on destruction and murder. At least that was what they had all first thought, even Molly. They had destroyed pretty much everything in their path. They were still cleaning up and fixing large parts of the ship, with some repairs expected to take weeks or longer to complete. The lounge where they were being held was emblematic of this: most of the seats were ripped apart; the batting covered everything, like a heavy snowfall. And as driven as they appeared to be by destruction, they were perhaps even more driven by their appetites.

They ate more food by body weight than what they did as humans, from the limited evidence they had so far. Molly immediately guessed this was because of their highly increased metabolisms, which had to be working overtime to maintain their accelerated activity and newly elevated body heat.

And in spite of the inactivity her ship had forced upon them with the cold temperatures, the parasitics' physical needs to fuel their accelerated metabolisms still meant lots more food. This explained their early rampage and eating of fellow passengers and crew.

Of course, they couldn't very well feed them live humans... She snickered at the thought of feeding some of the more problematic passengers, like Hans, to them. So they turned to raw meat, which seemed to be the only food they'd eat. But this changed fairly quickly after the first day. And it made complete sense.

As was the case with mammals in the wild, when their body heat was threatened, and after they had satiated themselves, they were forced to find ways to maintain their body temperature, and often go into a hybernative state. And that's what their parasitics had done.

But their parasitics were much more than wild animals. They were humans, and now humans with extra abilities.

She shuffled through her neatly hand-written pages, to re-examine her notes from last night.

It was her worst fear that these parasitics, who at first appeared to be just irrational animals, would start to use their cognitive abilities and apply them along with their new abilities.

And now they had proof that this was happening, along with one more new ability they had learned about last night. She needed to share these with Ted.

"Oh no!" she quipped, turning around to look at the clock by her bed. She was going to be late for her meet-up with Ted.

As she moved toward the bathroom to clean up, she shuddered at her thoughts about what these new discoveries would mean for all of them.

05

In The Air - Flavio & Vicki

"And when the whole thing was all sixes and sevens; Sean went all monkey on the zombies. And then Liz just smiled at him, as if it was the most adorable thing she'd ever seen." Vicki snorted at her story. But then something remarkable happened: her laughter exploded and seemed almost uncontrollable. But just as quickly as her jovial wellspring had burst, she cut herself off. "I'm sorry, I just loved that part..."

Flavio couldn't help but flash his own huge grin at her as she continued her narrative about some unknown scene from her favorite movie, *Sean of the Dead*, which he had never seen. And he wasn't really paying attention to her scene descriptions, much less trying to understand the movie she was describing to him. He was too enamored by her performance and her genuine enthusiasm. It was one of the most beautiful sights he'd witnessed in recent memory. Not that he could remember many beautiful things. But he could stare at her for hours.

It wasn't just that she was attractive—she certainly was. It was her passion and her laughter. It was so genuine and contagious. He felt the worries of his world drift away when she laughed. And she laughed all the time.

He had never met someone who was always in such a good mood, when he so rarely was in one himself. Sure, she had her down moments, like everyone else and most especially lately. But hers never lasted very long before she'd bring up some funny anecdote from her past or from a movie that taught her some life-lesson; something that had meaning and why the world was a better place than all of them thought because of that little snippet of human understanding she'd uncovered from something otherwise so trivial.

Flavio knew if the world was a better place, it was because of her being in it. Period.

"Are you even listening to me?" she asked, her face still wrinkled in a happy grin.

No, he wasn't. At least not completely, but he didn't want to generate a frown from her lovely face. "So why you love movie about zombies so much?"

"It's not the zombies really. I mean come on; the whole zombie-thing is pretty lame. You see, it's not about zombies; it's about the friendship with your mates and it's about love in the worst of times and it's about looking out for one another, all told through Sean and his girlfriend Liz and his best friend Ed. And I'm reminded of this often... with you and me."

"So that makes me Sean?" He glowered at her, not really meaning it the way he said it, and knowing the unintended connotation of what followed. But he didn't mind.

"Only if it means that I'm your girlfriend." She smiled and reached out and touched his hand.

At any time in the past, at a moment like this, when a woman would try and get close to him, Flavio would head for the exit. But nothing in him was yelling, "Run!" Quite the opposite. He wanted this, too.

He returned her smile with his own and covered her much smaller hand with his. Then he turned somewhat serious. "You know I have no girlfriend since my wife died."

His mouth started to dry up a bit. And he felt droplets of perspiration slide down his neck and puddle around his collar. For any normal adult male it would have been nerves causing this. Sure, he was a little nervous, but not for the reasons most men sweated during these moments with someone they were attracted to. And at the same time he felt confident he was exactly where he should be. He was mentally preparing himself to head down a road he hadn't traveled down in a while. He was about to dust off an old emotional road map that he had folded up many years ago and put away for safekeeping.

He *would* unfold it now.

He *was* ready.

He was the one that asked her out on this "coffee date," even though she used her own credits to purchase their coffees in the MDR. Every passenger was allotted one cup of coffee per day as part of their daily sea rations. He told her that it was sensible they'd share theirs together, in the open area of the Solarium. It was far more than common sense that drove him to ask her on this date.

"I do know this," she said softly. "We'll take this as slowly as you need."

"Don't need slow. Life too short." He abruptly leaned over the table, almost knocking his half-full cup of coffee over, and kissed her. It was the first time he had kissed a woman since his wife.

He sat back down and was greeted by the same captivating smile that he now knew he would look forward to every day, no matter what that day brought them.

Then he remembered where he had to go and his whole demeanor changed. "Sorry. Have to go."

Vicki looked at her watch. "Oh yeah, your new job. Do you know what it is?"

"No, but it better be good or I complain to captain."

Flavio squeezed her hand again. They exchanged quick grins and he dashed off.

Jessica

"I think you're all set, Jessica," proclaimed Deep, his grin stretching ear to ear. "You now have all of the ship's video feeds available on your console." He stepped away from her console to give her room to approach and give it a try.

Jessica returned a weak smile and approached her console before she halted. She already knew how to work the controls and trusted that if Deep said it was fixed, it must be fixed. She really didn't want to play with it right now, like he wanted. She just wasn't in the mood.

She attempted a smile again. "Thank you so much, Deep. I'll test it out later, if you don't mind."

"Oh sure. I know you have lots to do. I'll come back tomorrow and help you with anything else you may need."

"Hey, what about engineering? We have a long list of things that need fixing." Niki scowled, her words almost sounding like grunts.

Deep stared at the woman who was much taller than him—most non-Indian woman were—acting a little stunned by Niki's hostility. "Ah, Bu-Buzz," he stammered, "...is working on these, I think. I'll ask him when I see him later today." He turned back to Jessica, his facial features softening again.

"Anyway, I'll see you later." Deep's all-white smile re-enveloped his face. It was a nice face, and in spite of what was going on, it felt reassuring to have someone looking out for her.

"Thank you, Deep. You're a life saver," Jessica answered. "And thanks for the coffee."

"Sure," Deep said under his breath, while he grabbed his small bag of tools and beelined it to the bridge exit. And just as quickly as he had entered, he was out the door. It felt to Jessica as if some warm Indian breeze had blown through the bridge and was then gone in an instant.

"You know that boy just wants to get into your pants? Of course, he's not the only one." Niki flashed her cohort a mischievous grin.

Jessica glowered at Niki. Deep's infatuation with Jessica was widely known around the ship and Jessica really didn't mind it. He was sweet and a good friend, and she needed friends right now. She also didn't mind the chiding from others, including Niki. Except now, when each day was filled with a greater realization that she would probably never see her family again. She reminded herself that it was just Niki; this was the way she was.

Although Jessica had rarely worked directly with Niki, since Niki's position originally kept them on different decks, she was recently reminded why she didn't care for Niki: it was her acidic personality.

That and the fact that she's so damned butch.

That's when she was hit by what Niki meant by the second part of her statement. With this and seeing the knowing grin on Niki's mug, which then grew upon recognition that Jessica had just caught on to her pass, Jessica turned beet red.

"Ah... I..." she stammered. "You know I'm straight... and *married*, right?" Jessica held up her ring finger to buttress her argument. But the small diamond in her engagement ring, under the bridge's muted light, barely glinted a rebuttal.

"Hey, Sunshine, don't get your dainty little panties all bunched up. I'll stop hitting on you. But Deep is another story. He brings you his coffee allotment and then goes out of his way to make sure your console works, when so many other things on the ship need work. Just saying, you're going to have to do something about him."

Thankful now to be on this otherwise uncomfortable subject, but off one far more uncomfortable, she quickly answered. "Deep is sweet. He knows it's been a tough time for me."

"It's tough on all of us," Niki chortled. "But I suspect it's toughest on the guests who now must work as crew."

06

New Crew - Hans

"This sucks," Hans huffed. He reexamined his list, once again counting the number of cabins they had left to do. "Forty, forty-one... We have forty-one more of these damned things. And we've already been to this one before."

"Yeah, but then we're all done with this project," Frans stated, a little too enthusiastically.

"Sure, but then the captain will make us his personal slaves on something else. Don't forget we're supposed to be guests of this cruise line, not workers. I wouldn't have gone on this cruise if I had thought we might be forced into working. And all because we have special gifts."

"You mean because we're infected."

"I still don't believe that. We've been given special abilities. Though I would sure like some of the other abilities too. You know, like the super strength that that tow-headed woman has. Then we wouldn't have to take any more crap from the captain."

"Just knock on the door," Frans said, obviously annoyed by the whole conversation.

"Fine," Hans huffed back. He balled up a fist and thumped hard on the solid cabin door. "How do you say this *Schlitzauge's* name anyway, little brother?"

"I think, Ya-kO-bus," Hans read it phonetically and partially nodded his own acceptance to his pronunciation.

The door opened with a light squeak, and a single eye revealed itself through the dark slit. Then part of the man's face.

"Jes?" asked the sleepy looking mug attached to a single blinking eye, still shrouded in darkness behind the door.

"Are you Yakobus Wahid, currently working as a room steward on deck 7?"

"Jes... What is this about?"

Hans gave an exaggerated sniff, immediately crinkling his nostrils like he'd taken a whiff of something malodorous and then turned to glare at Hans, who nodded affirmatively back at him.

"Congratulations." Hans handed Yakobus a pre-printed piece of paper. "You've been given a new cabin, one much nicer than someone of your status would have normally been given."

Jaga

Jaga looked again at the piece of paper to confirm it. He'd examined the damned thing maybe a hundred times already. And each time he did, it made less sense than it did the first time he looked at it.

"Here it is, little buddy," he said to Taufan, "our new home."

He didn't understand why he had to move in the first place. There was nothing wrong with the arrangement he currently had. He liked having roommates. And since

Asap went all crazy and disappeared and Catur was gone, Yakobus and he had more room than ever before.

Now he was forced to leave his home of several years. No explanation. No reason. Just some big German dude and a smaller version—probably brothers—who showed up unannounced at his door last night. They were part of the new crew: guests recruited into service by the captain.

Jaga's first thought was that he was about to be fired for having a ferret on board, and for the trouble he caused. But nothing was ever said about this. Just the late-night knock on the door. Yet that wasn't the most bizarre part of the German brothers' visit.

After they had knocked on his door and confirmed he was in fact himself, they then did the most peculiar thing: they sniffed him. The two brothers then looked at each other, acting like he had body odor or something—even though he had just showered—and then nodded at each other. Then the big guy said to his brother, "Number 3626" and his brother pulled out a sea card from a box, handed it to Jaga and said, "Congratulations Jaggamashi, you're now in cabin 3626. Enjoy your new quarters, but move in by early tomorrow morning."

It was all so strange.

And he wasn't the only one. Many of the other crew—the ones who had been around for a while—were moved as well, some to this side of the ship and others to a cabin more forward.

"It makes no damned sense."

Now he was going to be living here, in a guest cabin, very much like the nice guest cabins he cleaned... or rather, used to clean, as he was also told that he was going to be given a new job too. Apparently the guests, or rather new crew members, would be cleaning their own cabins. There were more important jobs each of them would be doing. Though he couldn't imagine what else the captain would have him do.

He wondered who would visit him in the middle of the night to deliver that message. And what sense did it make to take him away from something he was good at? And he loved it too, seeing his guests happy during their vacations. He had received a lot of praise from corporate about this and it was the reason why he was given so many cabins to service.

He wasn't good at anything else. He never had much use for school and he didn't have any skills, other than taking care of his buddy. "Right, Taufan?" He scratched the tuft of fur below the ferret's mouth to encourage a response. Taufan gave a little groan. Jaga took that as a "Yes!"

He pulled the new sea card that he was given from his pocket and slipped it into the door. He was almost surprised to see the lock turn green and click open. Pushing in on the door, he was immediately dumbfounded. This was a giant room, far bigger than what he and Taufan needed. Why would they give him this big room, for no reason at all?

He looked down at his ferret, almost expecting help from him with this quandary. Taufan bristled in his arms: his buddy was asking to be released. No doubt he wanted to examine the room for himself.

"And look Taufan, you have a window."

Jaga allowed the cabin door to slam shut and then he let go of his ferret.

Taufan burst out of Jaga's arms and darted across the room to the large window, immediately enthralled with the island they were fast approaching.

Maybe he should look at this as a positive. Maybe a little change was good. "Why go to all of this trouble unless it was a good thing?"

Taufan chittered his response at the window.

It still didn't make any sense, but at least Taufan approved.

07

Flavio

He was on a quick breakfast mission for Thai food, if he could just find some. He needed to eat quickly to be done in time for his meeting, which he guessed other crew members like him would be attending, all to receive their new job reassignments, whatever they were. "Dammit," he cursed under his breath.

He found himself standing in front of the locked entrance to the crew mess. A recently printed sign—definitely not there yesterday—was taped to the door, to remind him and others why they were locked out:

From the Captain:

Everyone, including all original and new crew and all officers, is to take their meals in the Main Dining Room.

Flavio remembered hearing this, but it didn't register until now. *They damn well better have my Thai food,* he thought. But he knew that that had changed too, like everything else on the ship.

He smiled at this last thought, thinking of Vicki. Not all changes were bad.

Someone cleared his throat and Flavio turned away from the door to see a tiny junior officer standing behind him. The man's shoulders drooped under Flavio's shadow, as he hulked over the officer. "Sorry to bother you, sir," the officer said, peering almost straight up at Flavio. "I was just coming up to get you. You are wanted in the MDR by the captain. He's waiting for you right now."

All of this struck Flavio as strange.

He had thought he was meeting in a group, all to receive their new jobs from someone far below the rank of captain. He certainly didn't expect a private audience with the captain himself.

And how did this junior officer know he'd be here? The officer had said, *"I was just coming up to get you,"* which must have meant that he was coming up to his new cabin, since he was no longer in his normal cabin on this level, having been given one of the guest cabins, with a fantastic view and a great bed, several decks above them.

Then it struck him.

Flavio tilted his head upward, glancing at one of the hundreds of the ship's cameras mounted on ceilings throughout the ship. He nodded his understanding at the one less than a meter away, peering down at them.

But there was one more unexplained oddity that Flavio just couldn't wrap his mind around. This officer referred to him as "sir." Since Flavio was not an officer, he should have just been referred to by his last name, Petrovich. That was normal decorum on an RE ship, unless that had changed too.

Flavio recast his gaze back down to the diminutive officer. The man was patiently waiting for an answer or some sort of acknowledgment. "Thank you. I go now."

It was all Flavio could think of saying. His mind was having difficulty keeping up since so much was changing, so very rapidly: he had actually slept an entire night for the first time in memory, he didn't have a headache, he felt genuinely happy and to top all of this off, the captain of his ship was waiting for him.

Flavio shook his head, turned and started toward the MDR. He heard the soft shuffle of the junior officer's feet behind him when he entered the crew stairwell. It was obvious that the man had a mission to make sure that Flavio made it up to see their captain. Flavio was going to make sure the man was going to have to work a little to complete his task.

Some things don't change, he thought to himself, as a smirk crept onto his face.

It didn't take long, because Flavio double-timed it to the MDR, his destination. A part of him wanted to see if his shadow remained glued to him, though he wasn't sure why. And afterwards, he felt a little silly for doing this.

One doorway later, he stepped into the MDR. Behind him were the sounds of the diminutive officer hacking up a lung. Flavio chuckled to himself.

If I were in charge of crew exercise, you would be the first person who would have to run laps, he thought. His smile-lines moved higher.

Flavio found the captain right away. The man who only a few short days ago was the staff captain until he was elevated in title when his superior was brutally murdered by the parasitics. Jean Pierre stood up from his chair and greeted Flavio with a broad and welcoming grin.

"Flavio, thank you for meeting me on such short notice. I know this may seem like it came out of the white."

Flavio wasn't sure what the captain meant by this, but he heard the captain often said things that didn't make sense.

"I wanted to personally thank you for all that you've done the last few days. Your tireless work has been above and beyond. I would have preferred doing this more formally, out of respect for your recent contributions in saving this ship and so many people on board. But we have little time. And I need you now."

Flavio was taken aback by all of this, still standing and facing his superior, when he realized the junior officer that had been dogging him, still breathing heavily, moved into his periphery. The officer handed Captain Jean Pierre a small box and then moved away.

The captain turned back to Flavio and held out the case, now opened. It had officer bars in them. He looked back up at the captain, whose smile had grown ocean-wide.

"Flavio Petrovich, you have been promoted to Second Officer, effective immediately. And I would like to offer you the position of Deputy Security Director... Assuming you want it?"

Flavio was flabbergasted. This was Director Wasano Agarwal's previous position, before they found the then security director killed a few days ago.

Another crew member appeared from behind him—Flavio never remained this long with his back to a doorway. For the first time in recent memory, he was startled, actually flinching a little. The man was from laundry and handed Flavio a fully pressed officer's uniform. Flavio mindlessly took the uniform while staring at the captain, unsure what to say or how he should react.

Before all of this happened, when he was just a lowly waiter, rarely noticed by any of his superiors, he would have been sure that this whole presentation was all a way for corporate to reward him without giving him the raise that he'd deserved for all his years of service, but never got. And that was because he was already at the top of his ranking, without being an officer. Then he considered the truth, the real truth about their situation.

Neither he nor anyone else would ever be getting paid again, certainly not from a corporation made up of people who were either dead or crazy and running around the head office, murdering and eating their fellow corporate executives.

Flavio shook himself from his mental meanderings and saw the captain was waiting for a reply.

"Guess my overtime work paid off," he quipped.

The captain chortled. "That and your unique skill-set, which are needed far more now than they were in your previous position... Can I take this as a yes then?"

"Yes, of course, sir. I am honored, Captain." Flavio firmly shook the captain's hand.

"That's wonderful. Now, I apologize for the lack of ceremony, but we just don't have time for such niceties now."

Flavio was happy for that. He hated recognition ceremonies, which he had always thought were set up more so for recognizing his superiors who loved to self-congratulate each other and hear themselves make speeches. This was better. Much better.

He wondered what he was supposed to do next, his eyes wandering down to the captain's table, where he had stood up from. There at his place was an empty coffee cup and a half-eaten Danish. There were other place settings at the table. And he had kind of hoped to have been invited to sit with him and have a meal as well, but knew that was asking for too much.

"I'm sorry I cannot join you for a meal. And I'm afraid you'll need to be brief as well. As part of your first assignment, please change into your new uniform and at zero-eight-hundred, you'll need to meet us at the deck 1 port-side gangway. That's forty-five minutes from now."

08

Speed

T ed sat enveloped in a bubble of his own personal disquiet. He stared into the large space of the Solarium, lost in thought. With his Cubs baseball cap tugged down tight around his head, the bill covering all but the day-plus stubble carpeting his chin, he was almost unrecognizable, unless someone stopped and really took a look at him. Incognito was preferable at this moment, because he was too busy dealing with what felt like an immense crush of weight bearing down on him. It was the summation of all the ship's worries and his knowledge of how bleak their future currently appeared. Even though he tried to convince himself otherwise.

Assuming they were able to make a deal for fuel, they'd eventually run out. Then what? And food was going to be their bigger problem, even if they didn't part with much of it, which they most assuredly would do if they were going to make a deal for the fuel.

And assuming they were able to solve the insurmountable problems of their fuel and food, how could they survive this world now owned by the parasitics? He didn't even dare allow his thoughts to fall onto his wife, TJ. Each time he went down that road, he'd eventually drive off it, into a ditch of despair, heading down a hole of hopelessness, where his psyche would be crushed beyond repair.

Then his bubble of blues was pierced.

Some lumbering idiot clobbered into his table, jostling the two cups of coffee on top, sloshing out some of their coveted contents.

Ted shot his glare upward, a fusillade of profanities loaded up behind his tongue, ready to be launched at the person who did this. His lips were pursed, his nose drawn up. Then he held his breath.

"Oh dear me. So sorry, Ted," Dr. Molly Simmons gasped. "I get clumsier with each day."

Ted's anger withered immediately. "It's all right. Please sit. I've tried to keep your coffee warm, but..." He pointed to the upside-down saucer resting on top of a coffee closest to the empty seat, drops of black liquid dripping from its edges.

"Oh, thank you. So sorry I'm late—don't get up."

Ted halted, halfway out of his chair, then lowered himself back into his seat, abandoning his effort to help her into the empty chair awaiting her.

He watched her slowly pull the chair farther out from the table, turn it toward her and then fall into it.

Just before she was done adjusting her seat, a couple walked by their table and glanced first at Molly and then at Ted. Ted could see the spark of recognition in their eyes, but he turned away before he'd confirm it and they passed by without saying a word.

It was another reason Ted didn't care to meet in the Solarium. This place was way too open. It may have been less populated than in previous days, since the cessation of food service in all restaurants except the MDR. And since most every passenger was given a job, there was less time for leisurely sitting and resting in an area designed solely for recreation. More than anything else, Ted was afraid their open conversations would be heard by others. But Molly liked this space. So this was where they met each day.

She argued that it was warm and the canopy of glass brightly illuminated the space, even with their recent days being heavily clouded over.

"Oh, that's so good," Molly said, taking in her cool coffee in short sips, as if it were hot. In fact, it had lost most of its heat a half an hour ago, when he brought their coffees down from the MDR for their daily meet.

"You're not drinking yours—say, you look tired... Are you all right, Ted?" Her ancient-looking features were twisted with concern.

"Yeah, I'm fine. And yes, I need more sleep. Speaking of sleep, what about you, Molly?"

"Me? Don't worry about me. I'll get all the sleep I need when I'm dead. I'm too busy for sleep." She took a big gulp of her coffee, her eyes still uncomfortably riveted on him.

"All right, then. So how are our monsters sleeping?"

Her eyes dropped from his, to the cup she was holding. "Well... that's why I'm late." She set her cup down and then looked back up to Ted. Her persona instantly changed from enthusiastic to something more serious. "As a scientist, I have to tell you I'm both excited and terrified by what we're witnessing. I cannot explain it, except to say..."

She looked down again, took a deep breath and then exhaled. She lifted her gaze back up to Ted's again.

"I think we're looking at the next stage of human evolution. Assuming I believed in macro-evolution the way it's taught in schools nowadays... Scratch that, *was* taught in schools."

Considering his own dour mood, Ted almost needed to debate her point about evolution, sensing—and needing—another sermon from her about God's providential hand changing the events around them in His favor, and theirs. He was just too tired to get into another weighty metaphysical discussion. He chose to buttress his own hopelessness instead, "All right, so it's survival of the fittest. So who's going to be the fittest in the end, us or them?" He knew the answer.

She smiled a little at his question. He was pretty sure that she enjoyed having someone who could engage her intellectually, especially someone who possessed a similar love for science, like Ted did. "Short term, we may survive this, if providence still chooses to lay His hand upon us, like He has so far."

Ted couldn't help but smile at this, knowing she would go there. *Maybe I wanted this discussion after all.*

"But long term, the future probably belongs to our parasitics." She cast her gaze back down, almost as if she were embarrassed to having just given such an ungodly forecast of the future, because surely God couldn't support these evil creatures over his beloved people.

And even though he knew she had to say this if she were being faithful to science, it still shocked him. Molly was someone who he'd come to know had a rock-solid hope in tomorrow, buttressed by her faith in a God that loved His children. Ted wasn't so sure about the whole creator thing.

He had admitted to her that he was much more agnostic than atheist. Until recently, he had always believed in the human condition, and that through science and the good nature of many, humankind would be able to figure a way out of this mess before something ended it for them. Even in his fiction, he offered hope for his characters. But it was getting harder to believe in humans when there weren't that many around anymore.

He realized Molly was watching his reaction to her words now. "I've been wondering the same thing. What recent finding makes you believe this?"

"Oh yes, I hadn't told you yet. As you know, we learn so much each day as we study them.

"We're already aware that parasitics have an ability to use their muscles and tendons like those of a chimpanzee, giving them, from our observations, two to ten times normal human strength."

"I think you told me it had something to do with our brains getting in the way of our latent strength, as a means to protect our bodies."

"Yes, think of all of the reports you've read of a meek housewife lifting a car off her injured husband, or the daughter lifting the farm tractor off her father and so many other instances which prove this point: it's during times of extreme stress, or anger, that we can be at our strongest."

"And with parasitics, that's all the time, except when they're hibernating," Ted added so she knew he was following.

"Precisely."

"Okay, so what's the newest revelation?"

"Yes, sorry. You'll recall we've observed the parasitics hibernating in cylindrical groups that rotate periodically, sending those on the edges to the center, so as to maintain their body temperatures above the ambient temperature in the lounge."

Ted did remember this and found it fascinating. "Yes, I do. It seemed odd, but made sense when you first reported it. I was worried that if enough of them warmed up too much, our efforts to lower their body temperature would fail."

"And until last night, they seemed to remain in this rotating hibernative state, efficiently transferring their body heat to the others—"

"As if they were waiting us out, knowing the low outside temperatures were not going to last," Ted added. His dour mood was kicking back in again.

"Perhaps."

"You said, "Until last night." What happened last night?"

"Two recorded events, which have me troubled. The first occurred yesterday morning. Each cylindrical parasitic pod has kept one parasitic in the center, so as to warm up its temperature even higher. We only noticed this because yesterday, one of the parasitics darted from the center of a pod and tried to attack one of our guards on morning feeding duty. It was close, but our guard retreated behind the door, just in time."

"That shows strategy. Not something we expect from them," Ted interjected.

"Precisely. The second event which has me a little frightened is actually tied to the first. Last night, at the start of the second feeding, it happened again. Like the first attempted attack, a parasitic leapt from the center of its pod. Also like the first, it was a little clumsy and not particularly fast. But this time, halfway up the aisle, it literally shot up the remaining distance like a cheetah. I have never seen a human move that fast before. I had Mr. Deep rewind and replay this part over and over again, because I just did not believe what I was seeing."

"So you're saying they're becoming not only stronger than us, but faster too?" Ted's stomach was a boiling cauldron of acid right now.

"Precisely. Of course, this is just one incident, but I think you understand why I'm so worried now."

Ted thought about the repercussions of what this meant to all of them. It was too awful to consider right now. Parasitics with lightning speed?

TJ rapped on the window with two knuckles, generating a loud enough sound on the other side that it startled the store clerk. The man was self-jolted from his seat, dropping the clipboard he'd been holding.

He snapped his head in TJ's direction and then yelled inaudibly, "We're closed."

She knew what he said, even though his voice was almost completely muffled by the glass. But she wasn't taking no for an answer. So she acted like she couldn't hear him.

She mouthed, "What?" and raised her arms up as if she didn't know what he was saying.

The man violently shook his head and abruptly returned back to his work, yanking his clipboard from the floor, and continued to examine it and his inventory. At least, that's what she guessed he was doing.

Her anger grew. She hit the glass harder this time, causing the whole frame to shake. She was pretty sure if she struck the glass just a little stronger, it might break. *Don't want to do that more than once,* she thought while glancing at the broken window panel to the left of the door, now covered by plywood.

The clerk rose from his seat this time and stomped over in her direction, his shoulders stiff and aggressively pointed at her. As if he were going to win this showdown.

She almost guffawed at this.

The clerk plunged his metal key into the lock, turned it and cracked the door open. "We closed. Not sure when open again, but you—"

It was pure reflex, because without thinking, her hand shot through the door crack in a blur—much more quickly than she would have thought herself capable—and grabbed the man's forearm.

His eyes went wide and he looked down at his arm, convulsing with a jerk when he saw that she was clutching him, almost like he didn't know it was her who had a grip on his arm. He attempted to tug away, his face twisting into comical proportions as he pulled with his whole body. Her hand remained, an immovable vise clamped around his arm.

Then she squeezed harder, just to demonstrate she was in control. But she felt his tendons beneath her hand about to give, so she loosened her grip.

"Owah. Why you do this?" he whined, his face turning red.

TJ had planned a much more diplomatic approach, but when this guy stomped over to the door, it pissed her off. So she abandoned diplomacy for something more dramatic. And now she was short on time and just wanted what she came here for.

With her free hand, she pulled off her sunglasses and glared her scary eyes at the man. "If you don't let me in and give me what I want, I'll snap your arm off and eat it for breakfast." She said this deadpan, not really meaning it. She really had no desire to eat this man's arm.

The man's giant white orbs welled with tears and he tried once more to unsuccessfully yank his arm free.

Then she let go.

The man tumbled hard to the floor and he tried to desperately waddle away from her.

TJ snapped her sunglasses back on, slid into the shop, closed the door and locked it, using the key still inside. Then she glared at the man, who had shrunk into the recesses under a display of Regal European T-shirts.

"Look, I was just kidding about hurting you. I just need one thing. Give me that and I'll go away. I promise." She flashed him a smile to show she was sincere.

The man glowered at her from behind the T-shirts, hesitant to trust this offer, seeking comfort behind the clothing.

"Ya-ya-you promise to la-la-leave, if I give you what you want."

"Absolutely." She flashed a bigger smile at the man, like she meant it. In fact, she actually did: she was done dealing with this little man. If he didn't help her, she was just going to look and take what she wanted herself.

She glanced around the store and quickly saw the display. "Right there, that's all I need. Please get me that. I'm late, and then I'm going to accompany the captain to get us the fuel our ship needs. *Please.*"

The man tried to right himself, but started to fall back over again.

Again she reacted so lightning-quick, lunging forward and yanking him up, she even surprised herself. The man squeaked in amazement, again drilling his tear-filled eyes at her, like she was some sort of freak. Now she genuinely felt bad for putting this man through such terror. "Sorry, thought you were about to fall. Just trying to help."

She let go when he felt steady on his feet. He backed away from her and moved toward the display she had pointed to.

"Yes, that's what I want." She motioned past him, her smile leading the way.

He turned to the display, anxious to get away from this crazy woman.

Once he was at the display case, he wasn't paying attention and drove his knee into it, sending two other table-top displays onto the floor. "Dammit!" he huffed, and glanced at TJ, who remained in her place.

"What color?" he asked almost inaudibly.

"Blue."

The clerk reached inside, snatched two boxes from under the glass, and marched over to her, holding the boxes out in front of him like a shield of protection. "Here are two sets. Pa-please go now."

She accepted the boxes, unlocked and then backed out the door.

"Thank you for your help."

09

Meet Up

Ted stood, arms wrapped around his chest, his back holding up the room's aft wall, while tapping a nervous foot to the floor. She was late.

He looked at his watch—that he had never worn, until a few days ago—to confirm this. It was ten minutes past their meet time. This really annoyed him because it meant that he had less time with her before they both had their duties to attend to. They had so little time together these days.

He drilled his eyes through the all-glass conference room door, catching glimpses of people flashing up and down the aft stairwell, a few feet away.

She was never late before...

That was before all of her changes. He was the one who was usually late. It was his wife who reminded him constantly of his appointments. It was one of the reasons why he started wearing his watch, a gift from her a while back. When she had recommended he bring it on this trip, he questioned her about it. "Who wears watches anymore?"

"Remember, you won't be carrying your phone with you everywhere, and I don't want us to be late for shows, or our dinner with the captain."

"That's what I have you for," he told her. He was only half kidding.

"But I might not always be around... I may be lounging at the pool while you're writing. Please bring it."

It seemed like a little thing back then, barely a few days ago. Now every decision they'd made, and would make from here on out, felt doubly important.

An attractive blonde, about TJ's height, breezed up to the door, and he held his breath. But it wasn't her. To confirm this, the woman moved quickly past the door.

When he called her this morning on her house phone—he was allowed certain privileges being a member of the wardroom, including use of the house phones, which were still designated for emergencies—she at first didn't sound interested in meeting. He recalled this conversation too... "Good morning, how are you?"

"Fine," she said, absent all emotion.

"Are you sleeping?"

"Some."

"Can we meet?"

"I have to help with the fuel negotiations."

"You know that I know that. Please, I need to see you."

She paused for a moment, and then her tone changed. "Yes, I'd like that."

He had remembered this conference room was kept empty for important ship business and that it wouldn't be used just before this parley with this guy on an island who had fuel. So he set it up here.

Finally, he saw her slowly come up the stairwell and stop a few feet before the door, where she gazed inside and saw him looking back at her. It was hard to see her clearly, because the door was covered with smudge marks, probably from people looking in, and a recently erected sign on the other side that said, "This room is reserved indefinitely for the Bridge Crew."

She approached the door and pushed it open, and that's when he could see all of her.

He immediately had a flashback of the sexual dream that turned into a nightmare this morning, recalling both his arousal and his terror all at the same time. His heart raced again.

She looked absolutely radiant in her usual outfit: compression shorts and short-sleeve running shirt, complemented with color-coordinated running shoes; blond hair pulled back into a crisp ponytail; nose-plug winched around her nostrils, and its skin-colored tether loosely ringing her neck. She wasn't wearing her necklace, but she said the clasp had broken and she was afraid of losing it now.

He noticed right away two monumental changes in her appearance since the last time he had seen her.

First, her skin glistened a radiant brown; she'd been rapidly losing melanin, causing her skin to look a more deathly pale shade each day. But the biggest change was her eye color.

They were blue.

Not her normal blue, but not red or pinkish either.

Her smile made his heart sore. She seemed genuinely happy to see him.

And then she did something unexpected: she stepped up to him, wrapped her arms around him and squeezed him tight.

"I've missed you," he said into her ear.

"Me too." Her voice was nasal-sounding. She was also sweaty, like she had just completed a run.

He gazed into her eyes for just a flash and kissed her. That's when she went rigid and pulled away.

"Geez, you'd think we could afford to turn the air on in here," she joked, probably to cover her change. But her voice too sounded strained.

"You know, the whole fuel situation..." That's when he saw her cover-ups.

Her eyes weren't really blue; they were purple: she was wearing blue contacts, which couldn't completely counteract her red eyes. And her tan was from a bottle and not real. He could see now she looked more gold-colored than brown, like he had originally thought. He glanced at his hand that had clasped her shoulder and noticed some of the tanning cream had come off. He rubbed it around his fingers for further confirmation.

He glanced back up at her, but his gaze drifted higher, catching what he thought were a couple of white hairs hiding behind the blond strands in her well groomed eyebrows.

"Guess I could never fool you, Ted. Does it look that bad?"

"No... I guess a part of me wanted to believe that you were the same. You know, before your changes."

"Yeah, me too. But we both know I'm not. I'm completely different than what I was before all of this."

The truth was a bitter pill that he didn't want to swallow, but now he was forced to.

They held their silence for an uncomfortably long period of time. They had never had an uncomfortable moment of silence between them before, savoring each other's presence so much that periods without conversation were just as glorious as those infused with rapid dialog. That had changed too.

"I love you, you know," he said.

"But that's not enough anymore."

There it was. The fact that he didn't want to admit, but she put it out there. It was like a knife thrust directly into his heart. "Just don't give up on us."

"I haven't. In fact, knowing you are there is what has kept me... human."

At last, something to hold onto. They weren't lost, yet. He could still hope that she held on, as long as she remained "human."

There was a loud beep-tone, followed rapidly by another one. This was the prelude to an announcement. Before the apocalypse, these were often ignored because they were usually just outside of earshot and it was known that each was some sort of fun declaration about the day's drink special or an upcoming show. Now, the announcements brought him anxiety, even those he already knew about.

"That's the captain, telling everyone to get inside and to remain there until after we have concluded the trade and we've left the port."

"It's also why I have to go," she said.

He knew this too, but he didn't want their time to end, especially on her last hopeful comment. Then he considered what she was about to do.

"Please be careful." He thought about Molly's comments about the parasitics maybe having super-speed. "You may have new abilities, but you can't outrun a bullet."

This comment made her stop—she was already headed to the door. "Are we expecting trouble?"

"Ahh..." They weren't, but he was still skeptical of the whole thing. "No. Just promise me you'll be careful and not take any unnecessary chances."

She flashed her purplish eyes his way and gave him a slight smile. It felt genuine. "I promise. Bye."

She turned and was out the door. Gone.

10

The Parasitics

Whaudeep Reddy floated to the door and opened it just one second after Molly's faint knock on the other side. He didn't want her to wait long without protection. The area around the deck 8 Monitor Room, like most of the ship, was secure. But after everything that he'd seen, he didn't want to take any chances with this nice, elderly woman. So many images of violent murder were welded permanently inside his head, replaying themselves over and over, day and night.

"Oh my, you're so kind. Thank you for moving so quickly, Mr. Deep."

Deep offered an arm to help her inside, but she refused and hobbled under the aid of her odd-shaped cane. Once she was inside, he stuck his head out the door, to make sure no one else was there. His skin bristled at the thought that another one of those parasitics might be dashing down the hall, all because he wasn't at his seat watching for them, and warning the ship. He hadn't slept much worrying about missing the next attack. And with all that he'd learned from Dr. Molly's and his own observations, his anxiety grew with each passing day. Something was coming. And it was coming soon.

He checked in both directions: of course, the hallway was clear.

After securing the door, making sure it was properly latched, he turned to watch and wait for Dr. Molly to take her seat. *"Shuffle-thump, shuffle-thump,"* she worked her way to the chair beside his. The one with the two plumped-up pillows to comfort her aching bones.

Deep thought that she really should have an escort when she made her way forward, across the span of the ship, to the MR. With her reviewing tapes and making notes about the parasitics as often as four times a day, and for hours at a time, he was worried for the woman's health and safety: it would be so easy for her to trip and fall on her way to the MR.

But all his proposals for assistance were resisted by her, often with her stating adamantly that she didn't need any help, nor did she feel it was right to bother anyone else with such a request. Even when he offered to come and escort her himself, she said, "No!" And that it was her call, not someone else's. He at least got her to agree to call him first when she was headed toward the MR. That way, he could watch her like a hawk from his MR chair when she started her trip to the MR, just as he also did when she left the MR. At least he could do that for her.

Deep couldn't help but appreciate the work ethic of this woman, who was probably older than his own grandmother. And it wasn't that she had great stamina, as he often saw evidence of her exhaustion, especially now. Each time they met, she looked more and more the part of the elderly woman. He knew it was her scientific drive to understand their monsters, coupled with a general feeling of alarm that they had a very limited window to do so. Regardless of her reasons, Dr. Molly Simmons was someone he'd grown to care for and greatly admire.

He flashed an unseen smirk at her back, as she was getting set in her seat. He didn't want to rush her. So he'd wait until she was done fiddling with her cane, even though he felt building apprehension at being away from his monitors.

It was almost zero-eight-hundred, which was their normal feeding time. But after yesterday's two incidents of attempted attacks, right at feeding times, they had moved this morning's feeding time up a half hour or so, to see if the parasitics were going to try something right at 08:00 or would they wait for the guard and feeder's entrance around 08:30? And with the new information from last night, which he hadn't yet shared with Dr. Molly, there was no way to know what they'd do next.

He could see she was done fiddling with the pillows in her seat.

"Are you close enough to the monitors, ma'am?" he said softly, just behind her.

She turned her head and shoulders back toward him and glared a look that said, "I'm not so feeble I can't move my own damned chair!"

He nodded and whipped around her, dumping himself into his own seat. He typed a couple of quick commands on his keyboard and waited for her to start the review of some of the key video snippets he had compiled. He'd already seen the live feeds playing on four of the monitors, including the main screen.

Before she'd start looking at the video, she would examine his notes scrawled on the clipboard which he had left in front of her: a detailed summation of any interesting developments since her last review, the parasitics' movements and any thoughts about what he saw. She'd given him instructions on how to write research notes about their empirical observations. And he tried to follow her direction to the letter.

He was anxious for her to get to the newest development, at the end of his notes, which both surprised and terrified him. But she always did a review of their previous notes first, to make sure she didn't miss something, before she worked her way to the most recent point. He waited for her to get to that place, studying her facial features, while his mind wandered, thinking about how much had happened and what they'd seen so far in the few short days they'd been observing their parasitics...

Once they had control of them, Dr. Molly had been tasked by the captain to examine all of the live and taped feeds from the four cameras they had trained in and around the Wayfarer Lounge, where the parasitics were being held: two inside the lounge, one covering the main entrance, and one on the back stage—it was pitch black back there, so it was as if they had no camera there. None of the feeds had audio, so they could only rely on the video and the first-person reports from the guards who watched the doors and the volunteers who fed these monsters.

Since they had locked the doors on the parasitics and turned down the air conditioning to keep it icy cold, sending them into a form of hibernation, they had gained a lot of knowledge about them from the two cameras.

Deep had been on watch almost the entire time and had reviewed every moment of tape himself, including those from Fish's short shifts. He also read every one of Dr. Molly's notes. So he knew exactly what was going on.

Until an hour ago, most of the parasitics were asleep and naked. But it wasn't always this way.

During the first day, after the temperature in the lounge had dropped, the parasitics then mostly lay in their places and fell into some sort of quasi-sleep. Dr. Molly explained it was similar to what bears do in the winter. She said it was a semi-hibernative state, where they were very aware of what was going on around them, but as long as they didn't sense a threat, they remained where they were.

She said this was occurring for several reasons: they needed the rest to replenish their energy; their bodies needed to fix what was broken or damaged; and they needed to wait until it was warmer, so that their body temperatures could rise to their new normal levels, which was considerably hotter than our own normal.

After the first few hours of that first day, something unexpected, but wholly explainable occurred: they started to cluster themselves into pods, intertwining arms and legs so as to almost become one.

By the second day, all their clothes had come off, apparently for two reasons, one very odd and the other sensible.

Deep's cheeks always flashed red when he thought about this, and he was enormously embarrassed when he was present with Dr. Molly while she watched this with him.

Almost all of them had copulated together, often with whomever they were next to. Dr. Molly suspected that most of the time it was not the normal partner they were on the ship with. At first, Dr. Molly said she had thought this was part of their innate desire to indulge in their primal behavior, based on who biologically had the greatest sex drive. But the longer she studied the parasitics' behavior, the more she said she suspected there was a purpose to this behavior: the parasites inside each host wanted their hosts to reproduce.

She said this was especially odd, since it didn't fit the T-Gondii's normal life cycle of trying to end up in the guts of cats, where they could naturally reproduce. So her hypothesis—he loved that word—was that the volcanic bacteria that spread world-wide had somehow mutated or genetically altered the parasites which were controlling their parasitics, along with most of the human and animal population of the world.

But their parasitics' behavior wasn't just filled with sleep and sex. They had witnessed several murders as well.

Like the sex, Dr. Molly at first thought this was part of each person's basic needs being exaggerated by the parasite. And that this was just the parasitic's period of rage being expressed by murdering another parasitic that was in its way.

When it happened, it was quick and violent.

What changed Dr. Molly's opinion, at least somewhat, was after seeing what they did with the bodies: each was eaten.

So even though parasitics were undoubtedly driven to kill non-infected humans and consume their flesh for sustenance, they were not opposed to consuming each other, if it was necessary. Dr. Molly later said that she believed they were choosing to kill the weaker of their group, perhaps those with mortal injuries.

Whatever the reasons were, it was too gruesome to watch. And like the sex parts, Deep often averted his head or partially closed his eyes so he didn't have to witness this. His own fear was that these images would become commonplace to him and at some point, he'd find them no longer disturbing.

Luckily for Deep, these two behaviors seemed to stop about as abruptly as they began, but they also couldn't really tell.

That was because by the end of the second day, the parasitics started to use their already-shed clothing to cover themselves, like a large blanket. It was then that they realized the parasitics were both protecting their body temperatures and maybe even trying to raise them. Several other interesting developments immediately followed.

The pods became more defined, with 20 to 30 parasitics coming together in an almost perfect circle. It was hard to count the exact numbers, because most of these were under the shroud of their shed clothing. And the lounge's two cameras could only see so much.

By the third day, it was obvious each pod had its own structure. And that was when they noticed the pods were periodically rotating those from the outside in and moving those on the inside out.

It was only last night that they'd observed that one individual parasitic was being kept in the middle of the pod. Dr. Molly guessed that it all had to do with retaining that parasitic's higher body temperature so that it could use its new abilities for something they didn't yet know. At the beginning of the fifth day of their captivity, they'd found out what that was. That's when the attacks came.

Dr. Molly had thought the attacks were random; at least, at the time it *did* seem that way. The two attacks were against the guards, who were there to oversee the feeding and protection of that area. Each guard was attacked during the feeding times, when the guards entered the lounge. The first attack almost seemed telegraphed, with the parasitic grunting its intention before it started moving. The guard had barely opened up the door when he heard and then saw the parasitic running in his direction. He simply slipped back behind the door and closed it before it could get to him.

The second attack was much more of a surprise. The guard entered with another feeding volunteer—a newly recruited crew member from the guests that volunteered for this duty—who carried the food. The attacking parasitic dashed from its pod, which was also closer to the intended target. And it did so, as told by the guard, without any sound. The feeder reacted quickly and ran back out the door, although he tripped over his own feet at the door's threshold and fell just outside the doorway. The guard was two seconds slower, having followed the same path, but he didn't see the feeder at his feet, causing him to tumble even harder. Luckily, another guard was able to secure the doors before the parasitic hit. But the falling guard sustained a broken leg and messed-up ankle. It could have been much worse.

This morning's attack, the third one was the most odd...

"Fascinating..." Dr. Molly said, obviously reaching the end of his notes. She turned to him with a slight smile. "Thank you, Mr. Deep, for such a concise rendition of the last few hours' events. Can you please play me the recordings of the last attack?"

He had the two main camera recordings all cued up and clicked a button to start the recordings.

"This is the pod, Dr. Molly." Deep tapped on the screen at the pod that seemed particularly active, bristling with movement under its clothes-tent.

It came from the pod farthest from the main entrance door. The parasitic leapt out of its pod, this time headed toward the port-side lounge exit. And like the other two attacking parasitics, it first wobbled when it rose while it gained its stride. But even more so than the last one, halfway to the door, it moved with blinding speed. That was, until it hit the door head-first. Both the door and the parasitic sustained heavy damage. The parasitic fell to the floor from what looked like a broken neck and never moved again. The door held, but the frame was bent at an odd angle and the door itself was partially twisted inward; enough that it exposed light from the other side.

This was very scary to Deep for multiple reasons. Primarily because it was a fire door: a solid steel protective barrier, and all it took was one former human to almost take it down.

She had him play the tape back twice and each time she "hmmmm'd" out loud, seeming to pick up a new thought or a new piece of evidence to support her latest theory, which he desperately wanted to hear.

"Did you report the door?" she asked.

Her question jostled him a little, because he had lost sight of the obvious: if that door was not impenetrable, then these parasitics could get out.

He didn't hesitate, flipped a switch, snatched the microphone and clicked it open, "Attention Maintenance. This is Deep from the MR. We need a maintenance crew to the port-side crew entrance of the Wayfarer Lounge. There may be a breach in the side lounge door, holding back the parasitics.

Deep's eye caught movement on one of his monitors and he let go of the mic button. The main monitor was set to live stream from the camera right above the main entrance, facing aft. The same pod that sent the dead parasitic to attack the door was bristling with new activity. And then one of them leapt out of the pod.

"Look Dr. Molly, it's happening again."

11

Ágúst

The man formerly known as Second Officer Ágúst Helguson gave the order to the pod: a short but rapid gagging sound, which he knew to mean several things to the pod he commanded. And like all decisions and thoughts, he considered this one and what led up to it.

As before, he was more of a manager now than a leader and he was fine with that. When he was a mere human, he commanded many people, but only after receiving his orders. There were times he made decisions as the safety director of the *Intrepid*, but even those were a programmed result of a problem he had already encountered or was trained for.

And the few times he didn't know the answer, he relied on those around him, unafraid of delegating the many tasks given him to others who would complete the task more competently than even he could.

His life now was really no different, even if he was very different. Just like before, he reacted to outside stimuli, as well as deducing what might happen and his mind—because of his knowledge—would automatically generate the result. But it wasn't just his learned knowledge at work. There was something else.

Another being inside his mind was calling the shots. But it wasn't so bad, because this other being also gave him certain abilities that he never enjoyed as a mere human.

Besides no longer having an upset stomach or an irritable bowel, problems which used to plague him constantly, he had lost all his fears. He had none now. For instance, he used to worry what others thought of him, sometimes spending sleepless nights contemplating what he said or did, or what he was about to say or do. Not any longer.

Besides lacking worry, he had lightning-quick reflexes, twice his normal strength, an increased intellect and excellent eyesight. And he never had to second-guess himself, because the parasites inside him told him what to do and when to do it. So did Eloise.

The woman known to her dead relatives and a few on board this ship as Eloise Carmichael now had a hold over him he couldn't resist. And he didn't really want to.

When Eloise first spoke to him, it was right after his changes started. It was a confusing time for him, as his mind was filled with such tumult. The ship was in chaos, his colleagues panicking and he just didn't know what was going on inside his brain and body.

It was the reflexive nature of his former personality, which was afraid of what they thought of him. He didn't really fear it, only what was going on inside of him. But when they saw his red eyes and reacted with such horror, he thought he needed to do something to help his ship be safe. That was his job, after all.

When the task of securing the anchor release was offered and no one volunteered, he did. He could prove to them that he was still the Ágúst Helguson they trusted and do his job. But then she called to him.

He still couldn't explain it now, as he thought about it, but when he was running to get to the anchor release, he could feel her in his mind. As he got closer, the feelings were stronger. And when he saw her, he disregarded all he knew and learned, giving it all away to her. She told him what to do and he did it, even though some little part of him told him it was wrong.

But then she was gone and so was her pull. And his human side, even though it was barely there, called him back to his duties. It was a horrible time for him, because he was torn by two sides pulling equally then and he didn't know what to do. He felt sick and tormented by good and evil. And he was so exhausted. So he sought rest and somehow ended up in this lounge.

That's when everything once again became clear to him.

It was perhaps his fatigue at first, then it was his need to eliminate the confusion—the being inside him was offering the answers—but once he was in the lounge, with all the others, he had submitted to it. And he'd found Eloise again.

Previous to his changes, he was uncomfortable with women, having had sex only once, and it went badly. He had believed that sex was something that you only shared with a married partner; it was not something to be done with someone you casually bumped into.

Yet, when they discarded their clothing—he couldn't remember who told him to do this, his inner being or hers—he found her and she him and never questioned it. As it was with every part of his becoming something new, innately he knew he was being called to do this, so it must be right.

Immediately, he felt an even stronger intuitive connection with Eloise. He seemed to know her thoughts and she his. This was when the greatest changes took place in him as he accepted everything the parasites inside him and she told him. This included his command over the others.

He automatically came to know a new language and they listened to him and followed his commands without question. Unlike his human life, where he second-guessed his every decision and worried that others did as well, he never questioned anything. It was what was commanded of him and so therefore it was what he should do.

Today, he had a new command, a new purpose for their people. He knew what they had to do and how to do it. And so before they expected any of the humans to enter the lounge for their feeding, he heard in his mind and he then commanded that one of their strongest test their strength against the fire door on the far side of the lounge. He knew from his time before this would be difficult. But he also knew that if the right amount of pressure were applied to the right point in the door, it would start to give. And so the command was issued and carried out perfectly.

They knew they could exit out this door and so all they had to do was wait for their next feeding to start the next part of their plan. That was now.

Eloise bellowed a long single grunt, jostling Ágúst from his contemplations. He was given what his next command should be.

Ágúst immediately gave a series of short grunts that sounded like a seal barking.

The command's recipient burst from the pod that had physically prepared him for this. He dashed to the door.

Ágúst didn't even look to see if he executed his command. He knew he would. It was time for the next part of their plan. He bellowed his next command, knowing that this would soon lead to their freedom.

12

Ship Reps

When Flavio turned the corner at deck 2, they were all there, waiting. They reacted to his arrival, their gazes rising to acknowledge him. He instantly felt out of place.

Before all of this, he was a waiter, for God's sake. And a damn good one. But by some twist of fate, he was now the second in command of all the ship's security. Worse, he was a damned second officer, now part of that clan of folks he used to revile because they cozied up to corporate, so as to garner all of the increases in title and pay that weren't normally afforded to the likes of other crew, like him. But that was before; now he was not sure if any of his previous perceptions of reality were correct.

He only knew that he now had a job to do and that his captain had asked him to be here and to do this job. And because he accepted, with God as his witness, he was going to do it. And he'd be as good an assistant security director as he was a head waiter.

I'll be better!

At least that's what he told himself until all their eyes fell upon him.

He fidgeted with the buttons on his new uniform as he closed the distance between them. His new uniform fit well, perfect even. It just felt weird to be wearing it and the bars that had to be paraded so loudly on top of each shoulder.

Waiting for him was the captain, Mrs. Williams, and his new boss, security director Agarwal, who now wore three bars on his uniform.

The captain spoke first, "I know introductions are not needed, as we know what Mr. Petrovich has done for all of us this past week. But I did want to recognize Mr. Flavio Petrovich for taking the role of assistant security director and joining us here today."

There was a short clap from everyone, as each scrutinized him.

This was absolutely the one thing he didn't want.

"Way to go, Flavio," TJ announced with a smile behind her sunglasses. He was surprised to see that she looked less pale to him, like she was dead before and had come back alive today.

"Thank you, Mrs. Villiams," Flavio said and then nodded at her. "And thank you, Captain and Mr. Agarwal. It is my honor to serve you and my ship."

"I believe you know how to handle this weapon," Wasano handed him an M4 rifle. Flavio could see Wasano had another slung behind his back.

Flavio accepted the rifle, grabbing the stock with one hand and the rail with the other; the butt found a familiar place underneath his pit. He pointed it at a crate on the floor, away from the group. "It's not like my dependable AK-74." He pulled back the charging bolt and examined it to see if there was a round in the chamber. There was. He let go, letting it slide back into its place, and flicked the safety back on. "But this will do."

Flavio slung the weapon to his back, the same way his superior had his. "What's our mission, sir?"

Captain Jean Pierre looked like he was going to answer, but then he stopped and motioned toward the movement coming from the stairwell. It was five other security personnel, who appeared to be joining them.

"Very good. Now that we are all here," the captain lifted his voice, addressing their whole group, "we are waiting for the all-clear from our OOD on the port-side swing deck, as well as Ted Williams, who will be our base operator on the bridge. So far, we have not observed any activity out on the dock. We can't tell if anyone is alive. It's possible the radio broadcast is just repeating itself and the people who broadcast the signal are either dead or have left. And in fact, it does appear that this town hasn't sustained the chaos, fires, or death that everyone else has. It looks like the town has simply been abandoned."

"Maybe they heard British chef Jon is here to serve them food." Flavio instantly wanted to take this back, while he had to forcibly hold back a snicker that wanted to come out. He was shocked that the quip came out of his own mouth. It was like his old self was rebelling, not wanting to give into his new position.

"Officer Petrovich, do you have a question for the captain?" Wasano asked with a scowl.

"Sorry, sir. Only wanted to know, if guns for people or crazies?" Flavio coughed once in his hand, hoping his misplaced comment didn't get him into too much hot water.

"Maybe both. We just don't know. Any other questions?"

"No sir. Thank you."

While they waited several long minutes for the all-clear, Flavio examined each of the people in their group of ship's representatives, starting with Teresa Jean Williams.

Normally she would stand out in a crowd, especially wearing the only thing she seemed to wear now, very tight athletic clothes. Compared to the three officers in their formal white on blue uniforms and the other security in their standard uniforms, she looked out of place. However, he knew Mrs. Williams was FBI, and he had seen her in action. And although he still didn't completely trust her because of her recent changes, she seemed uniquely qualified to be a part of this group.

He suspected that the security director was capable. Wasano had already proven himself pretty solid under pressure. On the other hand, he knew nothing about the other security personnel, but he suspected that none had experienced any extreme pressure, much less being in a fire-fight. What kind of pressure does security see on a cruise ship, except dealing with drunkards and minor rule-breakers?

It was then Flavio noticed that each of the security team held their long flashlights as their only weapon. The largest of them had a stun gun holstered to his hip. Flavio always suspected there weren't many firearms on board. Seeing just the two rifles appeared to buttress his suspicion. He also suspected that no one but maybe Wasano and certainly Teresa Jean—who carried no weapons of her own—had any firearms training.

At least I won't be accidentally shot by my own people, he thought. This was not an uncommon problem with troops in their first battle.

He guessed then, that their real mission was to show force and more importantly, to protect the captain. This he knew he would do with his life, if necessary.

Flavio understood that they were there to make a deal with the locals of this town, assuming they were still alive, by exchanging some food for their fuel. But he also suspected that these people were probably the local thugs who had taken control during the chaos. They probably then cleaned up any evidence of their actions, so that they could lure an unsuspecting ship in under the promise of trading for fuel.

What is it the Americans say... It's not my first rodeo.

Flavio thought back to his time in the Romanian Army. Even though the Russians were on everybody's minds, it was usually the local mob or Bratva, or "brotherhood" as the Russians called it, who were most likely to fire upon them, even if you gave them what they wanted. Flavio's fear was that this group had no intention of making a deal with them. So as much as he respected his captain, the man was not accustomed to these kinds of situations. Neither was the security director.

Flavio was beginning to feel very glad he was asked to accept this position as he might be the only one with the experience to deal with what could become a bad situation.

Their radios chirped at the same time. A female voice crackled through. "I see someone coming. Suggest you put your earpieces on."

Flavio didn't have one, but he watched the captain, security director and Mrs. Williams plug their earpieces into their ears and into their radios, silencing the static.

He was glad for this, because he wanted to be completely focused on what was going on around him. He had a sinking feeling that he was going to have to use all of his experience and skills today.

13

The Island

S alvadore "Sal" Calderon marched down the dock—his dock—alone. He wore his dress blues for this occasion and his reflective sunglasses, even though the sky was darker than normal.

He stopped when he was halfway down the dock and glanced up at the giant cruise ship ported in front of him. He couldn't help but smile. He was amazed at how his plan had worked out so well. He had hoped that he'd be able to snag maybe a freighter or at least a smaller cruiser or two. Never in his wildest dreams did he expect a cruise ship to fall into his trap.

The food problem was getting bad and if this didn't work, they were going to have to take more aggressive actions and attack one of the neighboring islands. Of course, this was fraught with much risk, as they didn't know what to expect from the other populations, whether they were affected by the disease or unaffected. He had minimal manpower and few weapons. That meant his people could be wiped out in even a small battle, regardless of their capabilities. The last thing he wanted to do was leave the protection of his island, over which he at least had control. He just had to satiate his ravenous people before things got desperate. So he had to explore all options.

With only a few men he could trust to carry out his orders, he had started the planning for an incursion into Ponta Delgada on Ilha das Flores, the closest island to them. It was less than half an hour away by the only boat they had which could make the journey. They would pull up to the port and blast away any competition with their large weapon. Assuming it was then clear, they'd raid the port of what they needed and bring back fresh supplies to his island. If none of his plans worked, the final fall-back was to abandon his island altogether. Even though it was worst case, he had to still plan for this.

But then they received the reply.

A couple of days after Sal took complete control of the island, he learned the world around him had completely fallen apart. So he'd come up with the brilliant idea of setting up a beacon; a repeating radio broadcast that offered up the one resource they didn't need but had lots of, heavy fuel. Only big ships, like freighters and, of course, cruise ships ate up the stuff. The P-114 military patrol boat they had taken burned marine diesel. They had plenty of this already. So with his radio rig at the police station, he set up his broadcast and went fishing, using his heavy fuel as bait.

After the tidal wave wiped out many coastal communities on this side of the Atlantic, along with many of the ships already at sea, he wasn't sure what was still out there. He figured there had to be other semi-protected ports or bays, like theirs, which weren't too badly damaged, along with their ships. And he knew it was possible to survive a big wave at sea.

When he received his first and only nibble, claiming to be coming from a cruise liner, he thought maybe it was a joke. Or someone else's subterfuge. But to hear that a giant cruise ship had answered their call was simply too much to expect. Although not familiar with this particular ship, he had seen other Regal European ships ported on Sao Miguel, plus he'd read enough about them to know there had to be at least 1000 passengers and crew on board. And that meant lots of food for his people.

When he spoke to the captain of the *Intrepid*, Sal did his best to make it sound like a simple trade. "We just need a little food for our starving island, and you can have as much fuel as you want." Sal suspected a captain of a luxury cruise ship would be naive and not expect anything other than what he had heard. Still, they would be ready if the crew of the Intrepid offered up any resistance.

He heard a foot-shuffle coming up behind him, knowing instantly who it was. Sal turned to see Tomas hurrying up the dock in his direction, and he was happy to see that Tomas was following his instructions to the letter: his young agent wore his cleanest uniform and wasn't carrying his service weapon. Sal knew he could count on Tomas setting up everything else as requested. He was a smart boy, who understood well the penalty for disobedience.

"Everything is set, sir," Tomas stated this like a private to his drill instructor, only without any exuberance.

"Good boy," Sal answered, turning back toward the cruise ship, waiting for its hatch to open, and for the fly to get completely ensnared in his web. He licked his lips with utter anticipation, savoring in his mind what his next meal might taste like.

"You really think they will go for it?" Tomas asked, his voice stoic and professional, as always.

"They're here, aren't they?"

"Yes, but what makes you think they will make a deal with you?"

Sal hadn't yet revealed the main goal of his plan to Tomas, much less the mechanics of it. It wasn't necessary and he was pretty sure Tomas would resist him if he understood their ultimate goal. His best agent only had to follow orders. And he was good at that. He had others, with far fewer moral impediments and unique skill-sets, like him, to do his dirty work. "Simple. I'm going to accept whatever they offer, in return for all the fuel they want."

"Isn't that kind of craz—" Tomas stopped himself, obviously seeing the wisdom in not infuriating what he must have perceived as his power-crazed superior. "I mean, wouldn't it be better to hold back some of the fuel, out of the prospect of getting another ship to come here?"

The poor boy was just as naive as everybody else in this world. That is, everyone who used to be in this world.

Sal learned long ago, but it was made even more obvious very recently, that whole world was populated with naive people, who never would have conceived that something like the Rage disease would appear and change everything and everyone. People were like sheep, never able to think past their next latte, or their next sexual escapade, or even their next paycheck. The world's population had been weak and ripe for conquest. And now it would be controlled by special people like him—those who had the abilities and weren't weighed down by the moral entanglements to use them, for their own purposes.

As much as he wished Tomas was of the same mindset as he, sadly he wasn't. And while Sal still needed the boy, he had to use care in not sending him over the top by telling the boy their ultimate plans. He knew Tomas wouldn't be able to handle it. Besides, Tomas would find out soon enough what they'd planned to do with the cruise ship. And when that happened, he'd either be on board or Sal would kill him. It didn't matter either way.

"Look, there's someone on that balcony, off the bridge. She's looking at us through her binoculars."

Sal had already seen the woman. His eyesight was far better than the younger man's.

He looked in her direction and waved a friendly hello to the woman.

14

Wayfarer Lounge

They had both been dumbstruck when the parasitic had leapt from its pod.

It was 08:15 and just like the last attack, a lone parasitic dashed from the same pod, closest to that slightly damaged rear door. But unlike its dead predecessor, it slowed down before hitting the door, holding up right before its fallen brother, who lay lifeless a meter in front of the damaged door. With one arm, it effortlessly snatched and dragged the dead parasitic back to their pod, where it discarded the body at the pod's edge and moved away. What happened next was horrific.

The Americans had something called Shark Week on one of their TV channels that fascinated Deep and several other crew. It was supposed to be real-life, even though much of it felt professionally edited—something he understood quite well. What wasn't edited were the videos of schools of sharks being chummed with fresh blood and guts. It was like this, but worse. And in a way, what they had watched seemed less real.

Almost immediately after the body was dumped on its periphery, the pod buzzed as if it were an angry beehive. The pod convulsed and shimmied upward, at first moving amoeba-like slowly as a single form toward the body. Then the form broke apart into its many individual parts, which swarmed their fallen parasitic. Each frantically pounded and tore at the body, separating limb from limb, breaking up their comrade into multiple pieces.

Deep dared not blink for fear that he was going to miss the tornado-like blurs on the screen. Seconds later, all the parasitics rose back up from where the body had been and then rapidly regrouped until the pod was whole once more. The re-formed pod then finally settled back down, although it still seemed to gesticulate in an almost anxious anticipation of another feeding.

Nothing from the dead body was left behind, except for an almost imperceptible stain that could have been easily mistaken as a normal part of the loud carpet.

Both Deep and Dr. Molly sat in stunned silence and were so completely focused on the gruesome sight in the left-hand corner of the main screen, that they had forgotten about the parasitic that initiated the feeding of one of their own and then moved out of their way.

But then they caught the flash of the lone parasitic, once again dashing off to the right. It was so fast, the camera couldn't resolve its ghostly image, until it collided shoulder-first with the damaged door. It bounced off, falling to the floor.

Both Deep and Molly waited breathlessly to see what the parasitic would do, paying no attention to the new damage done to the door.

"Look Mr. Deep. He's injured pretty badly."

Deep saw this too; its right arm was broken and bent at an odd angle. "But that's on the other side of where he hit the... What's it doing now, Dr. Molly?"

Deep didn't see her shake her head, keeping his eyes riveted to the same scene she was.

The parasitic rose from the floor, seemingly unaffected by its injuries, only taking a second to examine its target.

It then backed up farther and then sprang. It moved even quicker than before.

This time they couldn't see which part of its body hit first. Deep instinctively knew that it went for the door at its weakest point and this frightened him to his core. It struck the door with so much more force that the wall around it shuddered.

Without the audio, they couldn't hear the impact, but they could imagine it. The door was now bent far enough inward that they could see the emergency light, fixed to the wall on the other side.

Like the first one, this parasitic collapsed to the floor, perhaps suffering a similar fate, after serving its purpose for its fellow parasitics.

"Was he commanded to do that?" Deep asked, but he didn't want to hear the terrifying answer. It was one thing to have a bunch of wild animals reacting to genetically innate desires and inner demons. If they were only like other wild animals, they could control them because humans were always smarter than wild animals. But if the parasitics were thinking, calculating and able to call up any one of their group to use their superhuman strength and sacrifice themselves, without fear or thought, humans were doomed.

Deep stared at Molly, seeing her eyes darting around the monitor's screen, as if she were some old computer using all of its processing power to calculate what the hell was going on.

She obviously wasn't ready to output, because she was still silent.

"Look," she whispered.

He did, his eyes first searching the monitor and then finding them.

"Ma'am, what are they doing?"

Molly squinted to try and better see the two figures standing in the very back of the lounge. One was the older woman Deep had recognized as the one who was running around the ship naked, attacking many passengers and crew. She was the one they called Eloise. Standing beside her was Ágúst Helguson, their missing safety director.

Wearing what appeared to be layers of other people's ill-fitting clothes, they were standing against the farthest corner wall of the lounge, almost completely hidden in the shadows. Eloise was telling Mr. Helguson something, as if she were commanding him to do something.

Mr. Helguson nodded. Then the former safety director opened his mouth and appeared to scream something.

"Mr. Deep. Warn our security now." She scooted up out of her chair. "Tell him not to go in!"

It was too late.

15

Ted

Ted flipped the channel selector to security channel two, or SC2, to make sure no one from their away team or Jessica was speaking. He had thought he'd seen the captain's lips move. His radio speaker emitted nothing but staticky silence. With his eyes riveted on his video monitor, his thumb and forefinger tensed over the channel selector. His attention was elsewhere.

He wanted to turn back to SC1 to eavesdrop on the conversations between the guards just as they were preparing for the feeding of their parasitics. Molly had told him that they were going to do this later than normal, because of the two attempted attacks on their feeding crews yesterday. Since it was a few minutes after eight, he was anxious to hear what would happen or what was happening.

The split screen monitor in front of him flashed two video streams, which seemed to change little: one from inside of the deck 2 port-side gangway and one just outside of it. The outside view revealed maybe a third of the island's dock, just outside of their hatch. Nothing was moving there, except the occasional gust of wind.

The inside view showed the members of their ship's away team, which included TJ. Everyone, with the exception of his wife, shifted weight between their feet or incessantly fussed over their clothing. Flavio checked and rechecked his rifle before slinging it behind his back once more. Supposedly the rifles were a show of force, which the captain said he didn't believe they would need. Almost all of them seemed anxious.

TJ, on the other hand, was a sculpted statue of patience. The only part of her moving was her chest, constantly heaving for air to fuel her racing metabolism. Otherwise, she carried the look of someone impatiently waiting for their number to be called at DMV. In other words, impatiently annoyed.

All were waiting for the verbal thumbs-up from Jessica, who was watching from the port-side swing deck. He suspected this would happen pretty soon since she had already instructed them to put on their earpieces moments ago. That way, the team could silently listen to any alerts either Jessica or Ted gave them. Jessica was primarily the eyes for this trade, since she had a complete view of the whole port and what lay beyond it. Ted was a backup set of eyes on the cameras and to relay any relevant reports from anyone else.

Three members of the team, TJ, Jean Pierre and Wasano, had inserted their earpieces. Then they had Jessica and Ted each do a system check to adjust their volumes. Then silence. The next word would come from Jessica, letting them know it was time to go.

Ted was surprised when he had been told that their earphones didn't have mics on them: they had to speak into the actual portable radio transceiver, which had to be inconveniently lifted from their belts to do so. It seemed silly to have inferior equipment such as this. Even the standard cell phone comes with ear buds and a microphone for hands free conversations. Of course, the away team would not be conversing with him or anyone else on the radio, unless everything went south, and then it probably didn't matter if they had microphones in their earpieces or not. The captain, the security director and TJ would be listening in for one reason and one reason only: warnings. If Jessica or Ted saw anything that would be a threat, they would warn them. And the more Ted thought about it, the more that he was convinced that he was making more out of this than was necessary.

The trade *would* happen, because it had to happen. So surely they'd figure out a way to make it happen. Their situation was that dire.

When Ted arrived, after his meet with TJ, engineering head Niki announced to him that she was going to have to increase the temperature in the Wayfarer Lounge and several pre-designated cabins at least three degrees every fifteen minutes and that all electrical systems were off. Only their most critical systems were on and running on battery power. Further, if they left this port right now, they'd have less than one hour of propeller use, at ten knots, before they'd run out of fuel entirely. She said that was enough to maybe get them to the next closest island and that was all. They had to make a deal and it had to happen now.

Ted decided very little was going on in the two areas he was tasked to watch. And because he wasn't expected to say anything other than if he saw something wrong, and that wouldn't be until after they opened their hatch in a little while, he chose to switch back to SC1 and listen in on the chatter about the feedings. He would switch the radio back to SC2 the moment he saw movement from the away team. Until then, he wanted to hear what the parasitics were up to next.

Immediately he heard the anxious guards, who sounded like they were sending in their feeding team right now.

"—imple. You all ready, two?" asked a familiar sounding Brazilian voice.

Ted suspected this was the guard named Paulo that he had run into a few days earlier, when trying to alert then Captain Jörgen to the dangers in Gibraltar.

"Jes, one. We have your back."

Even though he was staring right at it, Ted was startled to see some movement on his monitor. The team must be getting ready to exit. He needed to switch back to SC2, even though the feeding was supposed to happen right about now.

"This is Feeding Team One. I'm ready with my feeder to go in. Going silent."

"Two here. We're silent."

Ted's hand found the selector, while he focused on his wife, as she held up her portable to her mouth. He needed to switch now.

"Attention!" a frantic voice hollered. "We may have a breach on the port-side—"

Ted switched the channel.

"—ed are you there?" TJ asked.

"I'm here. I'm watching."

He could see a female security guard, operating controls on a small panel rising up to her belly. She flicked a switch and the hatch began opening.

"I just wanted to thank you for meeting me earlier."

"You're welcome. I—"

"Let's keep the chatter down to only warnings from here on out. Okay?" the captain offered his soft reprimand.

"Yes, sir," Ted quickly responded. He could see TJ nod her acceptance as well.

"OOD, everything look good still?" Wasano was holding his unit up to his mouth.

"Yes, sir. It's all clear. I see two men. Another has joined the first on the dock after going into a small building at the other end. You're good to go."

Ted desperately wanted to switch back to the other channel to hear more about the warning.

"Ted, do you see anything out of the ordinary?" Wasano asked.

Ted wondered what the hell was ordinary, for comparison. "No. I see less than you do. I can't even see the two people Jessica mentioned."

Jean Pierre nodded and then held up his walkie. "We'll see if we can move him into your view." Then he added, "I want all eyes and ears on these people."

The three with portables all refastened them to their belts and waited for the gangway bridge to unfurl itself onto the dock.

Ted knew he had to stay on SC2 for the duration, as well as watch them, even though any of his efforts felt superfluous. But at that moment, more than anything else, he wanted to desperately hear about the breach.

16

A Deal You Can't Refuse

Jean Pierre strode to a stop, holding up at least fifty meters from the two men waiting for them. A quick glance at their exit confirmed that they were in view of the ship's camera. He wanted as many eyes on them as possible. But the main reason for his abrupt stop was to move the negotiations in their direction.

He'd read endless books about negotiating at the insistence of his father, who wanted him to take over the family business, and Jean Pierre knew that a big part of starting a negotiation was controlling the negotiating venue. The venue favored this unknown group, because Jean Pierre's people and their ship were in unfamiliar territory. And since the stakes of this meeting were so great, he thought he'd try to get things started by forcing these unknown men to walk to him. It was a little thing. But sometimes the little things made a difference.

The two men, midway on the dock, both wearing formal police uniforms, shot each other looks of surprise and then returned their gazes back to *Intrepid's* away team. It was obvious they didn't expect this.

Intrepid's security director, Wasano, took his place right beside Jean Pierre, with his weapon moved from his back to his chest. Having a weapon was mostly as a show of force, indicating that they had the means and the will to use force, if they needed to. Wasano whispered, "I'm glad to see they're both police."

Jean Pierre also had this thought. At least at first. Then his mind started a game of devil's advocate: *Couldn't these men have stolen their uniforms from dead police officers?*

If this were true, they were probably in big trouble. If not, they'd probably make a deal.

His mind wasn't done: *If they're police, why aren't they armed?*

Many European countries didn't arm their officers and so this alone wasn't strange.

But in a new world, where crazed animals and people could attack at any moment, wouldn't you have weapons?

He remembered the radio broadcast, where the man said that Rage hadn't touched his island. Still, he did expect them to be carrying weapons.

But...

Enough! he thought, no longer entertaining these ideas.

Maybe the opposite was true and these men were trying not to show themselves as the thugs anyone would have assumed they must be. Perhaps they were leaders, just like Jean Pierre, only trying to manage a crisis on behalf of their people. People were starving, from what their leader said on the radio.

One of the two police officers smiled from behind his oversized sunglasses—the kind he'd seen daily on the cruise ship, often worn by men and women twice this man's age. This man also had more ornamentation than the other and so Jean Pierre assumed that he was the other's superior.

The leader and the younger man beside him proceeded to walk in their direction. They were coming to Jean Pierre on his own terms.

The negotiations had begun.

"It looks like they have fuel, sir," Wasano again whispered, making an obvious attempt at not letting the wind carry his voice to the other side.

Jean Pierre had also seen the fueling barge on the other side of the dock when they pulled up to the port. "Let's hope it's full of what we need."

As both men waited for the two officers to arrive from their slow march, Jean Pierre admired the little town in front of them. It wasn't the usual touristy town, whoring useless knick-knacks to ships full of people. It still had the flavor of the more familiar Azores villages. But this one existed to serve only its residents, who were mostly retired, government employees like these two men, and a few others who must have had some sort of employment, though he didn't know what that might be. When the small military base, somewhere on the other side of the island, shut down a few years ago the town's employment engine mostly died with it.

He had never been here and doubted any cruise ships had before them. The dock was way too small for a ship their size. The *Intrepid* didn't really fit. They had to jerry-rig some of their mooring lines to the side of the ship to moor them to a buoy, just off the tip of the dock.

The small size of their town and its even smaller population mix might explain why Rage hadn't hit their island. It was a logical explanation.

Just then, something rubbed up against his leg, jolting Jean Pierre from his thoughts. He looked down, expecting a sickly looking rat, which were way too common for his preference around ports. Instead, it was a black cat. It purred away like a little motorboat, doing side-swiping passes against his leg. The cute little thing looked up at him and meowed softly. Then it ratcheted its head forward, hissed loudly and then scurried behind him, out of his periphery.

"Captain Haddock, I presume?" asked the clean-shaven leader, with a welcoming grin and an outstretched hand. "I am Vila de Corvo's PCP Police Chief, Salvadore Calderon, and this is my best agent, Tomas Novo, at your service."

"Yes, I am. Greetings Chief Calderon and Agent Novo," Jean Pierre replied, shaking each man's hand. "This is my security director, Wasano Agarwal."

"Ahh, a French captain? Thought all of you were from Iceland."

"Belgium, actually. Regal European has"—*his mind flashed, HAD*—"captains from all over the world. So tell me about your fuel."

"Ha-ha, right to the point. Okay…"

The man seemed very composed, as if he just didn't care whether or not they made a deal. But he also seemed to be hiding something. And Tomas, his police deputy, or what he called "Agent," looked decidedly ill at ease: the man's face was as serious as death and his eyes darted everywhere and nowhere.

"Here's the deal," stated the chief. "The fuel barge you see here crashed on our shore a few days ago, carrying in it heavy fuel and MGO. We don't need heavy fuel and we already have an ample supply of diesel fuel for our boats. What we don't have is food, and I'm guessing you do, looking at the size of your ship. So here's my offer. We want three-quarters of all of your food. In return you can fill up your ship with all the heavy fuel you want." His smile remained, seemingly a permanent fixture on his face when he wasn't speaking.

Jean Pierre knew that this was just the first offer in their negotiations. But he also knew that he couldn't really spare that much food and he didn't really have anything else to bargain with. He also knew that every moment he waited here brought them another moment closer to running out of fuel. And that surely meant they were doomed. He had little time to stand around wagging their tongues with back and forth offers and counter-offers. He needed to close this deal. Now.

"That's crazy. We're a cruise ship of 3000 people"—he had decided it was better to exaggerate their actual population—"and we're low on supplies already after being at sea for over ten days. If we gave you three-quarters of our food, we'd all starve in a couple of days.

"We'll give you one quarter of our food and we'll take not only all the heavy fuel our ship will accept, but also your MGO as well.

"That's my final offer."

Jean Pierre shut up and willed himself not to breathe another word before Calderon did. This was another negotiating technique he'd learned: the one who said something first usually lost.

"Would you mind if I speak to Tomas about this in private?" asked Calderon.

"Of course," Jean Pierre replied, still acting as if everything was fine, although he was now starting to wonder if he pushed it too far. He was prepared to give away whatever he had to, in order to secure the fuel.

Wasano leaned in and muttered, "Sir, can we even afford to give away one quarter of all of our food? With so many mouths to feed, I fear we'll run out without any other options for finding food."

Jean Pierre remained stoically silent and waited to answer his security director, while he carefully watched Calderon for some sign as to what they'd do next. Calderon instructed Agent Tomas something. This appeared to light a fire in Tomas, who then turned and ran back down the dock.

Jean Pierre still didn't respond to Wasano's unanswered question, as he watched Chief Calderon return. He had planned to explain his future plans to everyone in the next couple of days. But only after they had their fuel.

The chief's smile rose higher on his face. "I sent my man back to get help to unload the food."

"So you agree to our terms?" Jean Pierre asked.

"Yes, of course." The chief thrust out his hand.

Jean Pierre couldn't hold back his own smile and vigorously shook Calderon's hand. *The man has quite a grip.*

Only then did Jean Pierre realize he must have been more nervous than he thought, because his palm felt hot and sweaty compared to the chief's cool and dry hand.

He then saw a dozen men already moving toward them. Jean Pierre had two thoughts then. *They must have been desperate for a deal as well. And he should have offered one fifth of his food instead.*

"My men will come in and inventory your food. And maybe you can help us with the offloading?"

"Of course. My procurement manager has already prepared an inventory for you and awaits your men inside. And what about the fuel?"

"As you can see, it's already making its way. Prepare for it on your starboard side."

He could see that the barge had started up its engine and several crewmen were already untying the mooring lines.

Jean Pierre breathed out a deep sigh. He was actually starting to believe this was all going to work out.

Even before the black cat had darted from the captain's legs, Flavio was anxious. This had quickly progressed to worry.

Like TJ, Flavio had been asked by the security director to hang back from the "negotiations" and to watch for trouble. He had done this, scrutinizing not only his captain, security director and the other two, but also the several men flooding into a small building at the beginning of the concrete dock they were all standing on. He also eyed the men on top of the fueling barge, just a few meters away. He felt certain that something was about to happen, at any second.

Then the cat appeared by the captain's legs. At the time, he thought nothing of it, even though it was black—he never believed in the old wives' tales. It was when the cat reacted to the leader of this island group with a hiss that something in Flavio's brain said this was all wrong. He knew dogs were good judges of character and wondered if the same thing were true about cats. That's when something did happen, which he would have never suspected.

The cat dashed in his direction then, rather than scurrying past him, it leapt onto his leg. As if he was some sort of damned tree, it dug its sharp claws into him. Because he was trying to be hyper-attentive to his surroundings and he felt sure that something was going to happen, he tried to ignore the cat, thinking it would eventually jump down. Instead, it started to scale his leg like a kitty-climbing wall, each paw's needle-like talons pricking his skin with each slow pull.

Flavio released his tensed fingers from his rifle, slung it around his neck and rested it on his chest. His hands found the soft little creature and he gently encouraged it to stop its trek upward and to release. He knew if he yanked it off, he'd lose some of his treasured skin in the process. Surprisingly, the cat let go and slowly walked along his straightened forearm, purring its delight at him.

"Looks like you have your hands full with a new girlfriend," chortled TJ.

An uncontrollable smirk cracked his facade. "Yes, Mrs. Villiams. I have a vay with women," he said, purposely emphasizing his accent.

He let the animal down and silently cursed either the blood or perspiration trickling unseen down his pant leg. At least it hadn't done this around his white-shirted upper body, which would have shone through. He glared at the cat, which was indifferent and continued its purring and rubbing up against his leg. Then it parked itself up against his shoe, where it proceeded to preen itself.

"Now she has to take a bath after you're done with her."

"Ha-ha-ha." He was not amused, even if he couldn't help but feel something for the little animal.

"Hey Flavio," TJ huffed. "It looks like JP made a deal."

Flavio glanced up, forgetting his new friend, and saw she was right. They were shaking hands and the other police officer—if they really were police—was returning with close to a dozen men from the building at the other end of the dock.

Flavio leaned in closer to TJ. "Do you smell anything about these men or this place? You know, are they infected?"

She removed her nose plug again—he'd seen her do this a few times earlier in the ten-plus minutes they had been out there. She shook her head. "I smell you now, but barely. It's hard to smell anything with this stiff breeze."

TJ slipped back on her nose plug, just as the captain and security director returned.

"Okay, a deal has been made," Jean Pierre announced, sounding somewhat jubilant. "They're giving us all the fuel we need, in return for one quarter of our food."

"Sir, you don't trust them, do you?" Flavio interrupted.

"Doesn't matter, Mr. Petrovich. I'm asking you and Mrs. Williams to escort some of their men to our procurement officer, who is waiting for you on deck 1, in the refrigerated food storage area. You both will be my eyes to make sure they don't try anything... funny. We're almost out of fuel and as you can see, their fueling ship is already moving to our starboard side to begin refueling. So I want this to go smoothly but quickly. Is that understood?"

"Yes, sir," Flavio said.

"Aye aye, captain," TJ stated.

Jean Pierre smiled and then followed Wasano up the gangway and back onto the ship, while Wasano spoke with his refueling crew on his radio.

Flavio didn't care for the brevity of all of this. The negotiation, the execution of the deal. It was happening way too fast. No time for planning and no time to consider the consequences if something happened. But his captain gave him an order and he would follow it.

As he followed the two men inside, he heard TJ, behind him now, casually announce the details of the deal on her radio.

He had to admit, he was beginning to feel very glad to have TJ with him. He felt surer by the minute that he was going to have to rely on her more than he wanted to imagine.

17

Otto

"**A**re you sure dis is all right?" gasped Otto. The rotund German had to stop again to catch a breath and wipe off the sweat rolling down his face. His heart raced like a freight train moving uphill, and he wondered if he might suffer a heart attack if he continued at this pace.

"You work for me now, lazy tourist. You do what I say," his new boss, Bohdan, huffed back.

The two other black-jumpsuited crew members chortled their amusement at their supervisor ordering around the former guest of their ship. The insults didn't really bother Otto; he just wasn't used to this kind of physical labor. Most days, he sat at a desk at his office in Munich, where all the running around was done by the younger associates of König AG, his namesake engineering firm.

Now, he was the errand boy for these three mechanical crew members, who seemed like they were up to no good, even though they swore otherwise. But what could he say? He was literally threatened with being kicked off the ship if he didn't do his duties. And he assumed the captain supported this way of thinking, based on his public statement and having crew with these attitudes.

The man at the top is always responsible for his people's actions.

At some point soon he would have to talk to the captain. Not to complain. But to promote the fact that a man with his skills could be put to better use than running physical errands. He would need to do this soon though. Because he wasn't liable to live through this kind of work much longer.

"That's enough. Rest over!" Bohdan bellowed. "We don't have much time to complete our work."

Otto exhaled his frustration, bent over to pick up the full 5 gallon water bottle and pulled upward. His back protested with a stabbing pain, a threat it was about to go out or just a warning—he didn't know. Somehow he was able to hoist up the heavy bottle to his side hip with both arms. He took a wobbly step forward. Then another.

"Come on, lazy tourist. This way," his immediate supervisor demanded. Bohdan was already many steps ahead of him, the others in tow, beckoning their struggling new crew member forward.

Otto wasn't sure what they were having him do, but he felt pretty sure it was not part of their normal duties. He had lots of evidence for this.

Their entry to this restricted area, off engineering, was done with some stealth. They pretended to be nervously fiddling with some controls, near a small access door, making sure they were not being watched. Only then did they produce a key card—Otto suspected the one he was given wouldn't work on that same door—and entered the tight access way. Through this, they had made their way up and over to where they were now.

Twice they stopped because they thought they heard someone else in the metal tubular walkway, crowded with cables and ducking. When they realized it was nothing, Bohdan moved them farther forward, but they were always looking back behind them, watching and listening for someone else who was never there. These were not the actions of men just doing their jobs.

Otto decided it was better to bite his tongue. He'd do what they told him to do, and then he'd tell captain all about this. Maybe he could garner some favor by reporting what their errant crew members were doing in the dark shadows of his ship.

"Here," Bohdan commanded one of the two crew members; their names, also Slavic sounding, escaped him. And unlike all the crew before all this craziness started, many, like these men, no longer wore name badges. Otto first assumed they were recent recruits, like him. He understood that lots of the existing crew were being relocated to different positions and even different departments, based on the ship's needs. For instance, he had heard of room stewards going to engineering or wait staff going to mechanical, which was the suspected job path of these men. Except they at least had the right color uniforms, which he did not.

The crew member Bohdan had been commanding set down his tool bag, opened it up, and pulled out a small reciprocating saw. The other crew member, the largest of the two, already had a drill out, and started drilling holes into the top of a long span of aluminum tubing running along the confines of the small access hallway they were in. Otto was no expert on the mechanics of a cruise ship, but he knew this to be duct work for the ship's HVAC system.

The moment the driller finished making four holes, the other crew member with the saw began cutting from hole to hole. And within less than a minute, a rectangular cutout was made.

"Are you sure this will work?" asked the driller.

"Yes, have faith, my friend," Bohdan reassured him, standing about five meters forward from their newly made hole. "We will be safe again after this. Now, make your next holes here." He tapped an area a little more on the side of the same aluminum ductwork.

Once again, the driller expertly completed his work, this time drilling four holes in the upper-side of the tubing. And the moment he was finished, the other worker stepped in and sawed another square piece out of the tubing.

Two holes, but for what? Otto wondered.

Both Bohdan and the driller moved back toward Otto, near the first hole's location, where Otto was standing hunched over, still collecting his breath. "Okay Anton. You grab the water bottle from fat boy."

This insult bristled Otto and he was immediately reminded of the nursery rhyme taught to him by his mother after school kids picked on him for being overweight: "Stöcke und Steine brechen meine Knochen" (Sticks & Stones may break my bones), "aber Namen können mich nicht verletzten" (but names will never hurt me).

It still hurt.

Anton, the driller, who originally carried the bottle up the access way ladder, once again effortlessly snatched the water bottle from Otto, hoisted it up and over the ducting, above the first hole. Then he lowered it, neck first, into the small hole at the top of the ductwork. Gently he let go and the bottle's weight pushed down on the soft material, making it and the brackets supporting the ducting crinkle slightly. But it held.

He still had no idea what the hell they were doing there... *Creating some sort of flood in the ducting? It made no sense.*

"Your turn," Bohdan demanded. Then Otto realized Bohdan was speaking to him. "Take this." He held out a thick plastic bottle that rattled, which he must have pulled from the small satchel he'd been carrying, demanding Otto take it.

Otto did as instructed and waited for his boss' next command, not sure he wanted to know where this was going.

"Pay attention now," Bohdan instructed. "Don't breathe when you do this. When I tell you... Open bottle"—Bohdan demonstrated by pretending to twist open the cap—"and pour in 10 or 12 tablets. Then close. Then quickly move forward from here"—he pointed to the end-point of the access way, only a few more meters away—"and we'll follow you from behind. Okay?"

Otto wasn't terrifically worried at this point, thinking this was just some sort of stupid joke three men were conspiring to do together and he figured they were already saddled with Otto. So they'd get him to come along for the gag, making him the mule to slug the water bottle around for them.

But then Otto caught a glimpse of the bottle's label and he saw what it was. He glanced up to Bohdan. "What could you possibly need hydrogen phosphide for?"

"Not to worry, tourist. We just killing some pests," Bohdan stated resolutely. The other two giggled.

That's when Otto panicked.

18

Flavio

Flavio had two immediate problems upon entering the ship. First, his new friend the black cat had followed him onto the ship, shadowing his every step. More importantly, he didn't know any of the names of the four men and one woman who were security and were waiting just inside the ship. He wanted to get everyone set before the men from the island came on board to do their inventory and start the process of collecting the agreed-upon food from their ship.

Cat meowed much too loudly and Flavio immediately felt the prickles of what he was sure was the other security guards' scorn as they eyeballed their new second in command, who just allowed an animal to follow him on board.

"I need four security to remain here and stay on radio channel"—he turned to TJ—"what channel are we on?"

"It's SC2, sir," answered one of the two women in his detail, with a dark complexion and strong South African accent. "We were already instructed to remain on comms. Ms. Kashatri, Mr. Akashi, Mr. Ivanov and I will remain at this hatch, sir."

Flavio allowed his gaze to hover on the guard, surprised at how competent she was. He assumed most of these guards were not going to be professional after seeing the way their former security director ran things on this ship for the past year.

"Thank you, Ms..." his eyebrows raised up, exaggerating his question, as he waited for an answer.

"Sorry, sir. Violet Johansson, sir."

"Thanks again, Ms. Johansson. Can two of you also work the metal detector machine right now? I want to make sure our guests don't have any weapons."

"Yes, sir. We were instructed to do that as well."

In fact, Flavio could see that two had already taken their positions at the machine.

"Okay, I can see I not needed here. Could whoever is left come with Mrs. Villiams and me and escort their men down to deck 1?"

"Aye, sir" came from a heavy-set guard. Then all eyes turned to watch the men from the island approach and mount the gangway leading up to their hatch.

"Mrs. Villiams, could you go and stay out of sight, but smell each man after they come through metal detector? I have feeling about these men."

TJ nodded and without a word, stepped through the metal detector. It immediately emitted an ear-piercing beep-tone and she reacted to it immediately, doubling over and clutching her ears, as if in pain. Flavio squinted to see where in her skimpy outfit she could possibly be carrying any metal on her, while she scurried through and disappeared around the wall leading to the stairwell landing.

His newest friend Cat continued her incessant purring. He couldn't have this, when he was trying to do his job as each of the island men scaled the gangway single file. He didn't want Cat hurt, but he couldn't deal with it right now—not even sure what he'd do with it after all this.

Flavio scooped up Cat—*Vicky missed her cat and would love it* sprang to his mind. He held it out to a portable fabric curtain that was used with others to partition an area for private screenings of passengers who set off the metal detector. Cat grabbed hold of the curtain and began to climb up it, leaving small holes where each of its claws had been.

Flavio quickly returned to the exit and stepped up to the first man who had come on board.

"I am Flavio Petrovich, second in command of security for the *Intrepid*. I'm here to make sure your men don't get lost on way to and back from our food storage. Dah?"

"Ain't... that sweet... We have... tour guides," huffed the squat man, who looked homeless, but well fed: his thick jowls waddled as he spoke, stopping every other word to take in a gulp of air with his giant mouth; his huge belly protruded out from a stained T, which seemed several sizes too small; and he was entirely plastered in a thick sheen of perspiration and dirt. Each of the man's wide nostrils appeared extra flared. And Flavio caught a flash of something white inside, but the man turned before he could see better.

"Please proceed through metal detector. Then wait for me with your other men."

"So long... as we get... our food... mate," said the man, flashing a set of equally dirty teeth. He then lumbered, as instructed, through the metal detector. No beeps or anything. Flavio stood in the way of the next arriving man, while he watched the squat man continue into the hallway, scanning his surroundings. Squat man abruptly stopped, a smile slithering onto his mug at the entrance to the stairwell. Flavio knew right away what the man was leering at: TJ. Flavio felt his stomach turn when he attempted to imagine what the man's sewer of a mind must be thinking right now.

Flavio turned to and spat out a retread of his directions to all of the other men, who all nodded their acceptance, each then processing through the metal detector and each finally lolling in the hallway with the others.

Not once did the metal detector chime an alert. And TJ didn't show or indicate any sort of alarm. After the final man, she popped her head out from the wall's edge to look back; finding Flavio's gaze, she gave him a thumbs-up.

All appeared right, but Flavio couldn't shake the sinking feeling in his gut that they were missing something.

19

Entropy

Otto glanced again at the bottle and then back at the tablets he had just poured out into the HVAC ductwork, then at the three grinning goons: two preparing to run back to where they had just come and one trying with difficulty to yank the cap off the water bottle. The obvious intent was to release its contents down the ductwork, so it would make its way... *To the tablets.*

Otto was a civil engineer who built exquisite German bridges and perfect German roads; he was not chemist. But he took enough chemistry in his primary schooling to know when water mixes with aluminum phosphide, it will produce either toxic phosphine gas—often used on ships to kill rats—or if there's too much gas, or a flame introduced to it, an explosion.

Bohdan had told him that they were "killing some pests." He suspected that these goons were planning to kill the parasitics the ship was holding in the big lounge. There had been many rumblings by former passengers and existing crew about how twisted it was to keep monsters on board the ship. Some of the more vocal folks advocated poisoning their food, or just tossing them overboard. Part of him didn't disagree with the idea: the parasitics posed a huge threat to everyone on the ship and if all of the crew—including the new inductees like him—were able to vote on it, Otto felt sure they would have unanimously voted to get rid of the parasitics. He had even heard Bohdan mention a meeting last night that Otto now felt certain was to give this man the go-ahead to take this very action. But this much gas would kill many of the non-infected people on the ship too.

It was also then, during his brain's rapid-fire assessment, that Otto connected the fact that Bohdan instructed him to move forward after planting the tablets. They were planning on running back the other way, leaving Otto to die from inhaling the toxic gas. Otto would be their fall guy. The one they could point their fingers at as the instigator of this crime.

"Come on, Anton. Finish it," Bohdan yelled at the big man, who couldn't seem to get the cap off the bottle by tugging at it through the little hole they had made on top of the duct-work. *They weren't the brightest bulbs in the pack.*

But somehow he did. Otto could see the air bubbles shoot upward in the clear bottle, indicating that water was pouring out into the ship's ducting.

Otto knew at that point what was going to happen and there was little he could do to stop it.

Maybe one thing.

Otto subconsciously patted his left pocket to confirm the presence of one object he needed. It was there.

His next decision was his last, but it gave him much satisfaction: in spite of the captain or his crew's stupidity in assigning Otto with such menial duties, he alone was the only person who could mitigate the loss of life Bohdan and his crew were going to cause. Knowing this made it worth sacrificing his life for all those he'd save, even if he suspected no one would ever know he was the hero.

As quickly as he could move, he jammed the open bottle of tablets sideways into the hole, so that all of the tablets would come in contact with the water. He could hear the water's effect on the tablets he'd already poured out and white vapor began to billow out from the hole.

"Come on, let's go." It was Bohdan's voice.

"What about the fat man?" asked one of the workers.

Otto was already running in their direction. And because of Otto's movement toward the three men, each of whom had turned to consider the man and the question, all were momentarily puzzled enough by Otto's movements and hesitated.

It was just enough time.

"What the fu—" Bohdan breathed before being hit by all 122 kilos of Otto König.

"**P**ull back! I repeat, exit the lounge immediately," Deep hollered once again into his radio, even though he knew it was no use. The guards had explicit instructions to turn off their radios during feeding sessions, so as to not to risk startling or otherwise awakening the parasitics. Neither the guard entering the lounge nor the other two guards outside the main entrance would hear Deep's warning.

The radio silence was supposed to last from the moment just before they opened the main door to begin feeding until the feeding was completed and the door was sealed tight. Physically switching off their radios negated any chance that someone would forget and cause a loud tone or voice, or that some other crew member would call out on SC1. Their reasoning was that the other two guards were already monitoring through a crack in the main entrance, watching the backs of the two who were tasked with feeding the parasitics.

The radio silence was supposed to be for the feeding team's protection. But now that rule put everyone in jeopardy.

Deep hesitated with the channel selector. He wasn't yet ready to alert the security on SC2 because they were too far from their location and had their hands full with the trade out on the dock. That left the general security channel, SC3. If there were any other security personnel left who weren't either part of the away team or the feeding team, this is where he'd find them. Those team leaders who were not on shift were supposed to have their radios on and switched to this channel. That was assuming there were any team leaders left. Deep wasn't sure how many they had after the first wave of Rage took the lives or humanity of so many crew members. And those who were left, he feared, would be helping the away team. He'd try anyway, switching the channel from SC1 to SC3. "Attention all security, this is Monitor Room Supervisor Whaudeep Reddy. I have a priority one message for all security personnel: we need additional security support to the Wayfarer Lounge on the double. Repeat, all security personnel, turn to SC1 and report to the Wayfarer Lounge on the double."

Deep switched back to SC1 and repeated the same message he did before.

He expelled a monumental sigh, lowered the microphone from his mouth and fell into his chair. All they could do now was watch, hope and pray there would be no attack. Because if there was, this time, he didn't think they'd fare well.

From the main entrance camera, Deep and Molly could see an armed security guard, followed by the feeder, carefully move inside the lounge. From the inside, long-view camera, in the back of the theater, they could see the two men enter tentatively. The security guard had his rifle at the ready. His charge, the feeder, carried two heavy shoulder bags of raw meat: the only food stuff the parasitics seemed to eat now.

At least it wasn't people, Deep thought.

The security guard halted just forward from the main entrance camera. He raised his rifle to his cheek and gazed through his sights.

After the last two attacks, the guard assigned to feeder detail was given a rifle and instructed to use lethal force if he felt either his or the feeder-volunteer's life was in danger.

Molly didn't like this at all, but Deep was glad for it, especially right now.

They literally held their breaths and scrutinized both monitor views, hoping nothing would happen.

The guard, with his weapon firmly pressed against his chin, rotated his torso like a gun turret. He seemed ready—almost pleading—for any threat from the parasitics to give him a reason to pull the trigger.

Neither the guard nor the feeder seemed to have heard Deep's calls on the radio, nor the other two guards at the door, who Deep could see just through the crack in the main entrance doors. It seemed like business as usual, just tenser than previous feedings.

Deep's fingers were interlocked in a prayer-like death grip, now white with the tips angry-red. He mentally pleaded with them to finish soon.

The feeder had held up behind the security guard, who signaled with one finger, his okay to move forward. The feeder nodded, accepting the quiet command from the guard that neither Deep or Molly could visually make out, but knew was given.

The feeder took several quick steps forward, walking past the guard, who trained his weapon on the closest pod, only a few meters down the aisle, which led directly to the stage.

Heavy-breath—"Mr."—*another heavy breath*—"Deep?" Dr. Molly panted.

Deep exhaled a long chest-full of air. "Yes, ma'am." His eyes moved from screen to screen to screen.

"Are we missing some of our parasitics?"

He snapped his head to face her. "What?" He heard her. He just didn't understand the question.

She sprang out of her seat, leaned over the long desktop separating them from the monitors and tapped the main screen. "This pod is definitely smaller." She moved her finger an inch over and tapped again, "And so is this one... In fact, all of the pods now look to me..."

"Like they're smaller in size. I... Hey, you're right. But where could they..." His head snapped again in her direction and hers to him.

Together, they yelled out, "The stage!"

Deep pounded his keyboard with a computer command, sending the dark stage camera view from a smaller monitor to the largest one. The video feed showing the volunteer gingerly lowering his food bags to the floor disappeared and was replaced with one that was thick with blackness.

At first glance, it was easy to assume that whatever the largest monitor was displaying was devoid of any light, as if it were turned off. Deep even shot a glance down to the power indicator light, to make sure it was on.

It was still green.

Then they saw the blackness on the screen was actually bristling with some sort of activity, like flashes of static. They could almost feel it more than see it, because when they focused on a perceived ghostly movement, the screen was still black.

Then there was a painfully quick splash of light through the center-break in the curtains. For just a moment, it appeared as if there were a multitude of people standing up on the stage. Like the final act of some giant talentless show, involving all the ship's bad actors; a curtain call to a horrific ensemble, that wouldn't receive an encore.

Then it was gone.

All at once, the curtains parted wide and out poured an uncountable number of parasitics. A geyser of terror sprayed into the lounge.

They'd been assembling there, waiting for this moment; when the main entrance was least secure; when the guard and feeder were preoccupied; and all timed to occur after they had found a way to open up the other door.

They had planned this.

O tto held tight, not letting go of the men. He had his arms wrapped around all three. They kicked and punched, but he held on. Otto knew this would be his final heroic action, not that he was feeling particularly heroic at this moment: his mind was filled with revenge. He'd take these horrible men with him. He was most impressed that he had no fear and felt deep satisfaction knowing the other three did.

Gas billowed all around them. The three men in their black jumpers coughed and choked as they struggled to get free of Otto's grasp. And in their struggles, they breathed in more of the toxic gas. Otto wedged his eyes and mouth shut, holding his breath, not because he thought he would escape death. He was certain this was how it would end for him. He just wanted to make sure these men felt death's sting before he did.

Finally, as the men quickly succumbed to the toxic effects of phosphine gas, searing through their lungs, eyes and skin, Otto couldn't hold his breath any longer. It was time.

He let go of the three men, fluidly snatching the cigar lighter from his pocket, and held it out ready before he was forced to suck in a deep breath of the caustic fumes. I shouldn't have waited so long, he thought.

With his eyes still shut, Otto involuntarily thrashed. He felt vital blood vessels and maybe even some organs inside him begin to burst. He had maybe a second or two.

Otto had two final seemingly disjointed thoughts: this was a real-life example of entropy, as in this was the point in their closed system when disorder began; and he wished he could have taken out his cigar and lit it before this.

He clicked on his cigar lighter at the same time he flicked open his eyes to see what it would look like. The effect was instantaneous: his eyes caught the beautiful blue flame, followed immediately by an all-consuming white light and then nothing.

20

The Trade

Minutes before their boat shook from the phosphide gas explosion, TJ had been eyeballing the disgusting men from the island carefully, even taking in another whiff of each. But other than their hideous body odor—which made her wince—and their revolting sidelong glances at her, she couldn't find anything out of the ordinary. Yet she couldn't shake a feeling that there was something wrong with these men.

Before they started their trek down to deck 1, all their eyes were trained on either her chest or crotch, their hideous minds actively molesting her. She understood this and even expected it because of her chosen outfit. Still, it incensed her.

Pushing aside her anger, she focused on the first two men who boarded, but held back in the procession to the food storage: one was a stocky pervert with a bulging belly and other was skinny with a drawn face. They seemed different than the others in a way she couldn't place. She wanted to take just one more whiff of these two, to see if she missed something, but watching them ogle her spiked her anger further. And she was afraid if she did take another whiff, she'd lose control of her anger and just kill these men.

This caused her to question whether she was actually receiving some input from her heightened hearing, sight and smell, all instructing her that something was wrong. *Or is it the Rage disease in me, trying to wrestle allegiance of my senses so it can use them for its evil mission?*

The men followed Flavio and the ship's other guard down the stairs to deck 1 and then finally they turned onto the I-95.

The squat man at the end of the line continued to turn back and glare at TJ. Although all of the men looked like they'd lived on the streets this whole time, Squat was the most disgusting of the lot. His black-as-night eyes glared evil thoughts, while his tongue constantly protruded out of his muck-filled beard. And multiple times he'd made a lip smacking sound that turned her stomach. She was about to grab his flabby mug and pull it right off his stump of a body.

When she made the turn onto the I-95, she decided that however she was able to, she was going to have to kill this man first. That's when she was struck by how empty this place was.

The main artery to the entire ship, where its vital crew members circulated from every part of the ship, through its smaller capillaries, each carrying the life-sustaining resources or services that made this ship function, was dried up, as if the heart of the ship were no longer pumping.

In fact, she knew this was by design. The captain had ordered all crew to be in their places before these men entered their ship.

Up ahead, several crew were already speaking to Flavio, who introduced them to the men.

TJ slid by them all and found Flavio deep in the hallway where most of the refrigerated food was stored. He had stepped away to allow the crew and the men to inventory and transact their business.

"You look out of breath," he said to her, genuinely worried about her.

"I always look out of breath." This was true. She wasn't out of breath; it was just that she breathed much more rapidly than before. "I cannot place it. Either it's their smell—which is definitely off—or it's their mannerisms, or it's something else. But there is something wrong about these men. Especially those two."

She pointed at the squat and skinny man.

V lad Smirnoff—no relation to his favorite vodka that shared his name—knew he probably should have worn his clean jumper today, after seeing his fellow crew in their best. His mama drummed into him at an early age to always wear clean clothes because, "you never know if this was your last day." He had no idea how right she was.

Instead he listened to his best friend, who ranted, "To hell with them. I'm not dressing up for extra duties." Their extra duties were to assist with the refueling of their ship. They weren't part of the normal refueling crew, but everyone was pulling multiple duties and multiple shifts lately. He often didn't listen to Sven, who always mouthed off about corporate, but for some reason he did today. Part of him wanted to be rebellious, like Sven. The rest of him just wanted to be home.

Vlad stared out the porthole in their exit, watching the refueling barge tie up alongside them.

"Out of the way," commanded one of the normal refueling crew, who rudely pushed Vlad aside. He guessed it was to confirm it was okay to open up the door.

He glanced back at his friend, who was slouching off to the side, acting disinterested. Sven was always trying to act tough, whereas Vlad just wanted to get this job done. Especially now. The stakes were high, from what the captain told them: they needed this fuel; it was as vital to the ship as their own blood was to them. And if they didn't get this fuel, their situation was pretty hopeless. The captain didn't say that last part, but Vlad knew this to be true.

Without the fuel, they'd never get to the next port, much less make it back to their families. None of the crew had heard from their families in days. They had no way of knowing if their families were even still alive with everything going on in the world and on this ship, from crazy people, and crazy animals, to cities burning and chaos everywhere.

It didn't help to know, as the captain liked to tell them, that their situation on board was much better than the rest of the world. He suspected that might be true, but that meant his family had it worse.

Their ship was currently consumed by organized chaos, with short-staffing and passengers becoming crew to plug up the holes. It kept their minds off their families but it also added to their exhausting duties. Sven and he had to train two men and a woman earlier this morning while they did their normal engineering jobs. The woman was pretty bright and seemed eager to learn, even though she didn't speak Czech or much English (the only two languages they knew). Although she did teach Sven and him a few words in German. The other two men were a different story.

They ignored most of what Sven and he had instructed, nodding their heads occasionally, but often making comments under their breaths in German, which neither of them understood. He suspected they were unkind comments, because at one time the German woman said something scornful to the two, then smiled at Vlad and said, "Please make more teach."

Sven hit Vlad in the shoulder, shaking him from his daydream, just noticing that the door was sliding open.

"Ready?" Vlad asked his friend, who nodded back with zero excitement.

Their job was to help the others with the fuel hoses, which sometimes got quite heavy. They'd be setting up two hoses, one for each kind of fuel, going to two different fuel tank fittings on the side of their ship. Normally it was two Intrepid crew, assisting two or three crew of the fuel barge. But there were at least two or three times more crew members here today, all waiting to hop onto the barge and get the refueling done quicker than normal, as if they were racing against the prospect of the men on the fueling barge changing their mind.

He started moving with the others toward the gangway off the hatch, which was a narrow balcony-like walkway running forward from its opening. From there, they'd have to hop down to the deck of the barge and not fall off. Vlad was deathly afraid of heights, but even more afraid of falling in between the two ships and drowning or getting crushed to death. He felt his anxiety soar as he stepped outside and saw the drop.

Then, probably because he didn't have any time to think about it and the others pressing against him, he hopped the four or five feet to the barge as if it were a normal day's activity. He landed in a crouch so as to not damage his knees or tendons. Standing up straight, he looked back to see Sven was already behind him.

"Piece of cake," Sven muttered, although he often said this when it wasn't.

Vlad looked back along the span of the barge's deck and noticed many more workers than he expected. He counted maybe a dozen, even though there were usually only a couple of men needed to do this job. Even with double or tripling the workers to accomplish the task faster, it didn't account for the total number of personnel here. A couple of them wandered over to meet with the *Intrepid's* crew, who were already grabbing hoses. The remainder of the barge crew, if that's what they were, jumped up *Intrepid's* gangway and entered their ship. It made no sense.

"Come on. We're up," Sven said, slapping his shoulder.

Vlad caught the scornful gaze of his new superior, at least for this shift, who was waiting on them to help him lug the heavy hose. And so he trotted over to help hall it over to the connector fitting on their ship. Another oddity was that their supervisor was manning the hose, not the barge worker, which was usual protocol. Vlad turned back a couple of times to see if Sven noticed any of these oddities too.

"Don't you see it?" Vlad asked him and was surprised to see a man, who he guessed was one of the barge workers, in between Sven and him. The man wore sunglasses so he couldn't tell if he was staring at him or at where they were connecting the hose.

Then they stopped, with the *Intrepid* crew member who was their direct supervisor busily connecting the hose fitting and then giving the okay to the barge's control operator, topside and behind them. Their supervisor waved as if the operator wasn't paying any attention to him because his waves became more furious.

Vlad glanced back to find the operator staring at his shoes. Until there was a loud whistle—maybe from his supervisor—and the operator looked up, glaring hatred. Then the operator pounded something on a panel and Vlad immediately felt the flow of hot fuel running through the hose, through his work gloves.

Vlad checked again with his supervisor to see if it was all right to drop his portion of the hose, but then he did this anyway because the damned thing was getting hot.

Oddly, he didn't see his supervisor at all, like he had disappeared. Vlad was about to search for him when he heard a commotion behind him, followed by a gurgling sound. Swinging around to see, he found Sven clutching his neck, his face twisted in wide-eyed confusion. Blood was trickling out from his fingertips, like he had cut his neck or something.

In shock, Vlad was about to yell for help, when his attention was pulled to his right, were he was met by the toothy grin of the barge worker who had been between them. He held a large cleaving knife up, its silver blade coated in red. *That's Sven's blood on it!*

The yell, which was stuck behind his swollen tongue, erupted the moment the worker plunged the cleaving knife into Vlad's chest. Just as abruptly, it was yanked out and Vlad was kicked to the deck. He laid there in shock, his brain not fully registering or unwilling to register that he had just been stabbed and would die there.

He felt more like a witness than a participant to everything unfolding on the deck: a set of gloved hands pulled against his chest in a futile attempt to stem the blood flow; some Intrepid crew who had earlier come out to help were also lying on the deck motionless; the barge worker who had stabbed him was climbing up the gangway into their ship.

The fuel barge was all a ruse. They used it to penetrate their ship. They were all going to die.

Vlad maneuvered himself to see his friend.

Sven wore a death mask: his eyes blank and fixed upward in a perpetual gaze at the darkening heavens, his hands loosely covering his throat which still trickled blood.

Vlad knew that would look the same in a matter of moments.

He turned onto his back and glared at the sky.

The thick clouds churned above and rapidly darkened around the fringes. With each blink they choked off more and more of the sun's light.

Screams in the distance.

The blackness rained down upon him, enveloping him.

Just before his last blink, he heard an explosion.

The skinny man walked right into the refrigerated liquor storage area, as if it was his own personal stash. "Now we're talking," bellowed the squat man, whose hairy belly pushed farther out from the bottom edge of his sweat-soaked T-shirt. He strutted into the room after his buddy, like a passenger who had paid for one of the top suites and expected top-flight service, when TJ guessed he wasn't much more than a second or third-tier henchman.

Intrepid's procurement manager and his assistant in training followed from behind. She heard the manager argue about whether liquor was part of the trade or not and then the room went quiet.

"Where's the rest of their group?" asked TJ, swinging her head around.

"There were eight men total," responded Flavio, stepping up to one of the three open refrigerated rooms. He ducked in, stepped out, and shook his head.

TJ jogged over to the third room, looked in and then returned to Flavio.

A glass bottle shattered in the liquor storage room.

They dashed inside where they found Skinny, in the back, standing over their procurement manager, a clear knife being pulled from their man's chest. TJ knew he must have been hiding this and because it was plastic and didn't set off the metal detectors. Skinny made a motion like he was about to drive it back in. Squat, on the other side of the room, had the assistant by a shirt collar and was reaching for his own plastic knife.

Flavio reacted without hesitation, shooting Skinny once in the head, pivoting on a heel to take out Squat. But TJ already had him down on the floor, the knife kicked away and the assistant duck-walking the other way.

Squat tried to wriggle free, but she pushed him down harder. Then he laughed, bellicose-like. "It doesn't matter. You and your people will be dead soon enough." She drove her knee hard into the man's arm, snapping it with a loud crack. But rather than crying out, the man laughed harder. "Hah-hah-hah-ha."

"You think you can hurt me? No, I'm going to hurt you," he boosted.

TJ glowered at his black-as-oil eyes and sneering face. She was about to say something, when she caught only a flash of his other hand, swinging around, followed by the ear-rattling blast of Flavio's rifle.

The bullet shattered the man's left shoulder and he dropped the knife that he had somehow gotten hold of while TJ was torturing him. She felt the squat man finally give up the fight. His breathing escalated to the point he sounded like he was hyperventilating.

Squat closed his eyes and smiled a wide smile. "Oh yeah, you can kill me. But it won't matter." His voice was even sounding. Controlled.

He paused a long while, and both TJ and Flavio waited, not sure if he were about to pass out or what. TJ shook the man, like a ragdoll.

Squat flipped open his eyes. For just a moment, TJ thought they flashed red, before returning to their oily blackness. "While you're feeling me out, my men are taking over your bridge and will blow your engine so you can't go anywhere. And when we're done, I'm going to eat you two for breakfast, with a little hot sauce on—"

Flavio drove the butt of his rifle into Squat's face, his nose making a satisfying cracking sound. He went limp.

"I had enough of you," Flavio added.

TJ handed him her radio. "Have Ted check on the engine room and the refueling team. I'll head to the bridge. You go to the engine room. We need to stop these attacks."

"Wait!" Flavio warned. While holding the radio, he slung off his pack, reached in and grabbed his two Moraknivs, handing one to TJ. "Take this just in case." She accepted, sliding it behind her back, into the fold of her compression shorts.

He attached his to his belt, while re-securing his pack and rifle. Bounding up, he had the radio to his mouth, intending to start transmitting, when the whole ship buffeted and shook. A tremendous boom echoed deep within the ship's skeleton and under their feet.

That's when they both ran.

21

The Explosion

The explosion not only incinerated the four men involved in the giant fireball, it also blew apart all of the aft ducting, thus severing A/C in the ship from the midway stairwell to the very stern. The fireball melted much of the plastic jacketing which protected the wiring and cabling that ran the access-way. As plastic and other flammables continued to burn, the concentrated heat fairly rapidly melted off the remaining protective coating from the wiring connecting every system in the stern. Then various systems started shorting out and shutting down. The heavy-duty power cabling was the last to fail.

With little more to burn, the fire was out, but the phosphine gas continued to billow out from the aluminum phosphide dust still being exposed to the air coming from the incoming A/C ducting. The lethal combination of toxic phosphine gas and air conditioning would have been deadly to everyone in the stern if all the vents had not been closed.

This was by design, as Regal European programmed this feature into its ships to lessen the severity of a fire. The thinking was that if all venting were closed, the hot air and smoke from the fire couldn't travel through the air ducting, and there'd be less circulation of air, lessening a fire's spread.

As it turned out, most of the vents were already closed, so as to lower the load placed on the ship's A/C compressors until they had received fuel. Once the power was cut to the aft decks of the ship, the remaining vents closed, too. This combo may have saved a hundred lives from the effects of the phosphine gas, but it also saved the parasitics in the Wayfarer Lounge.

There was still some leakage of the phosphine gas, as vents were not completely air-tight, but the small amounts that found their way into cabins, although disturbing, would not be deadly.

With all the vents closed, the phosphine gas had nowhere else to go. So it continued to billow through the small, seven foot by seven foot access way. It moved forward, following the same course Otto and the other dead men had come from, traveling rapidly along and then down the tubular structure.

Originally used to kill rat populations, the phosphine gas then rolled down five decks until it held at deck 1. It grew thicker and thicker, patiently waiting for any unsuspecting rat or person to wander in.

The deadly gas only had to wait two minutes to kill its first of many victims.

"Are we under attack?" bellowed Ted. Alarms rang out and lights flashed all over the bridge.

"Captain," hollered Niki, ignoring Ted's question. "I'm losing power readings for all aft decks."

Ted instantly knew what this meant. No power equaled no air conditioning. No air conditioning meant the couple hundred parasitics they were holding were going to wake up.

"What about the AC?" Ted asked, thinking instantly that it was a stupid question.

"Compressor is still operating at twenty-five percent. But I can't tell if any of it is getting to our guests. If power goes out, vents close... I now have zero—repeat—zero readings coming from anywhere from the midway elevator going aft. So I have no idea if they're getting anything."

Wasano had popped in from the port-side swing deck, where he had taken over monitoring the dock from Jessica, so she could return to her station as OOD.

"Ted, get on the horn with all our security personnel on SC3," Wasano stated. "Let's get people to all decks mid-way and find out what happened." He said this and immediately called out on presumably another channel.

Ted had turned down the volume on SC2 to talk to the bridge crew, but when he turned it back up, he heard the frantic call from Flavio. He spun it to its max setting so that everyone could hear.

"—under attack. At least six men are headed to the bridge and there are others headed to the engine room. We are under attack. I am headed to engine room."

The captain flew to Ted's right and picked up one of the phone lines to another section of the ship. He was immediately speaking to someone.

"Flavio, it's Ted. Where's my wife?"

"Please contact refuel team," Flavio continued. "Attack came from there and food area. Mrs. Villiams is coming to bridge. I am—hold on." Flavio yelled something, followed by a single gunshot. *Bang.* "Sorry, must go," he said and disconnected.

Ted didn't wait; he flipped to SC3, eyeing Wasano hurry across the bridge to the starboard side. "Attention all security personnel. We are under attack from a group from this island…" Ted held open the transmission, but put his hand over the microphone.

"Wasano, did you catch all that from Flavio?"

Wasano was still moving toward the starboard swing deck. Opening the door, he barely paused, said, "Yes" and shut the door behind him.

Jessica marched to the left of the captain and even though Ted was not too familiar with the bridge, he knew where she was going. "Stop!" he hollered at her before she punched the ship-wide alarm button.

"I just heard on SC1 that the parasitics are trying to break free. Let's not incite them any further with that loud noise. Remember what happened with the birds."

Ted remembered he had the mic still open, wondering what he should tell security on SC3.

Wasano popped back in from the starboard swing deck, holding binoculars. He looked like he was in shock. "They're all dead," he huffed.

The entire bridge held its collective breath for a moment, considering what was just said, and then the frenzy continued.

"Ted," Wasano continued in his normally controlled voice. "Call E1 and tell all engine room personnel to exit out the aft crew stairwell to deck 3."

Ted followed his directions, letting go of the mic, shutting off his transmission and flipping the channel selector to E1, Engineering.

Ted transmitted, "Attention all engine room crew. The engine room is about to come under attack by outside forces, who mean to hurt you. Please evacuate the engine room immediately. Repeat, evacuate the engine room immediately through the aft crew stairwell and continue to deck 3. Go up the crew stairwell to deck 3 and await other instructions."

While the captain was speaking to someone named Ms. Johansson, Ted wanted to see and hear what was going on with the parasitics, as well as talk to his wife. But he couldn't do everything at once. He switched the radio to SC1 while he attempted bring up the cameras on his monitor. He typed in one command after another, but he couldn't find any cameras working in the stern.

22

Violet

When Violet Johansson first heard the dull thrumming boom, followed by the shudder underneath her feet, she dropped down to her knees. The memory of a terrorist bombing in Istanbul, during one of their ports of call, was still fresh in her head. Pretty quickly, she realized that this was different and she went into action.

"Mr. Ivonov," she bellowed, "please check the inside door again and make sure it's secure. Ms. Kashatri and Mr. Akashi, please secure the outside door."

"What was that, Violet?" begged Ms. Kashatri.

"I'm about to find out." Violet picked up the direct line to the bridge and pressed the plastic button. It immediately flashed red and her receiver made a dialing tone.

The plastic button turned solid green.

It clicked a connection, meaning someone picked it up.

"Port-side gangway, Ms. Johansson calling," she announced.

"This is Captain Haggard, Ms. Johansson. Are you all right?"

"Yes, Captain." She was a little surprised the captain himself answered and not the OOD or someone else. "We were just trying to find out what just happened, sir."

"We don't yet know, Ms. Johansson, but I would ask that you secure your area. And do not let anyone onboard without a second officer or higher's approval. Is that understood?"

She watched the gangway door shut, her team doing exactly as requested. "We are already secure here... Ah, sir. We also heard what sounded like gunshots. What can we do here, sir?"

"Hold on," the captain asked. Then she could hear voices from the bridge and the words "They're all dead" from her new security director.

Violet could feel goose bumps blossoming down her neck, in spite of her perspiring a lot. Then she started to shake. She was absolutely terrified by the time the captain got back on the phone.

She heard him take a deep breath before speaking. "Ms. Johansson, we believe the islanders are trying to damage our ship. Hold position. However, I do need one of your team to check on the starboard exit. The crew doesn't answer our calls. There may be combatants there, so be vigilant and be safe. If possible, secure that exit. If not safe, just report back with status."

"Aye, sir." She sucked in several breaths of her own before placing the receiver back in its cradle.

Then she turned to face her team.

They eyed Violet, their saucer-eyed faces were deadly serious. Expectant.

"I think we're under attack," she said. "The captain wants us to protect this exit, but he also wants one of us to check the starboard exit, which isn't reporting." She turned to the tall Russian. "Mr. Ivanov, I'm asking you to go, but the captain warns that there might be combatants there. Don't take any risks, but..." she paused. "If you're able to secure the outside exit, do so. Then return and report."

"Aye, Ms. Johansson."

Igor Ivanov didn't hesitate. He cracked open the interior door, waiting for Violet to come from behind and get ready to secure it behind him. When she was there, he checked the area just outside the interior doorway,

It was clear and so he slipped through, Violet immediately closing it and locking it.

Igor Ivanov felt the door close behind him. When he heard its lock click from the other side, he knew right away that this was a bad idea.

There was almost no place to hide. As the Americans would say, he was a sitting duck.

A good span of the port-side hallway, leading forward and aft, was open in both directions. The stairway landing was wide open and directly in front of him. And the opening into the starboard hallway and then starboard exit was right there as well, open all the way to the outside. And that's when he saw the dead crew member.

Igor immediately took cover behind the hallway wall's edge, in the event a bad guy came out of that gangway door or the stairwell or elevators. He also knew that he'd achieved one part of his mission of finding out the status of the starboard exit and their crew: it was unsecured and their crew was dead. But he was not to take any risks and moving beyond this point was risky. He knew he should have knocked on the door and retreated back to safety.

But then what?

Was he just to let these murderers do what they wanted? And how long could the four of them remain locked up in their area? And didn't this also mean that the rest of the ship needed help? He could not just do nothing. Then he looked down.

On his hip was his only weapon, a stun gun. Yet they had real guns—they had heard the shots. That's a fight he'd lose every day.

But there was no one in sight and his mission wasn't done.

Igor convinced himself to take one quick look at the starboard exit, close it and then return for a full report to the captain. Maybe then the captain would advise them how they could fight back.

Igor again checked the hallway aft and forward, before proceeding into the stairwell and elevator landing. He walked quickly, while still keeping an ear to anyone coming up from deck 1 or coming down from deck 3, just above. Other than a distant murmur below, he heard nothing else.

At the starboard hallway, it too was clear, so he continued into the starboard gangway area, holding up at the threshold.

Like his team did on their starboard side, it was here where he could secure this area with a large wall and doorway that slid into place. But that would have still exposed them to further penetration from the outside. He needed to secure that exit. In between him and the exit lay the bodies of several of his crew. Then one of the bodies moved.

Above a fallen crew member, another man was bent over... *eating him.*

It still didn't feel real seeing a person casually kneeling over and chowing down on another person, even though he'd witnessed this a couple of times during the last parasitic attack. But here was this man munching on a dead crew like he was enjoying a late morning buffet. In an unseen hand the cannibal must have had eating utensils too, because the blur of a clear-plastic knife appeared, swinging at the dead man's arm, cleaving off another piece of muscle.

Igor gasped. This he'd not seen before. He'd only seen them use their fingers and mouth to tear at tissue.

Just then the cannibal stopped, swung his head up and glared right at Igor, his red eyes ablaze.

Igor sucked in a huge breath. He must have made a noise watching this and now he was caught, backing up.

Equally surprising and new was the cannibal's speed, because no sooner did Igor turn a shoulder with the intent to run when the knife-wielding cannibal leapt off the dead crew-member and was there, vice-gripping him with one hand and plunging his clear plastic knife into Igor's gut with the other.

Igor acted on pure adrenaline; his stun gun out, he jammed it into the side of the cannibal's neck and clicked the button, releasing 60,000 volts into its carotid. The cannibal let go of Igor and the knife and pulled away slightly, causing Igor to fall onto his back, with the knife still protruding out of his gut.

The cannibal convulsed twice more, while standing, like he was doing some macabre dance routine. But then he rapidly regained control of his muscles and nerve endings, even though he'd received a four-second jolt, which should have been enough to knock down a moose. The cannibal came at Igor again.

This time, the cannibal-monster, with red eyes practically pulsing at him, led with his blood-coated mouth open wide, blaring an inconceivably loud bray. Igor attempted to scoot away, but the cannibal was too fast. Igor turned to his side to make himself a smaller target and to block with an arm, as the cannibal came down on him.

Once again, Igor's reflexes were his friend at that moment. And perhaps so was the cannibal's one-track mind, set on sinking his teeth into the Russian. Somehow, Igor was able to move his stun gun around and jam it into the cannibal's mouth as it tried to clamp down on his other blocking arm. He clicked home the trigger, this time holding it down as long as there was a charge left, and watched the cannibal dance some more.

It may have not been the best idea, but when terror and adrenaline are cascading throughout your body, your thinking is far from logical. With his blocking hand, he yanked the now red-colored knife from his belly and shoved it, with all of his remaining strength, into the dancing cannibal's neck. Then he let go.

The cannibal danced for almost twenty more seconds, violently writhing on the floor, before he was finally silent. At the same time, Igor felt very, very tired, even though he had a raging fire in his gut. He laid his head on the floor, staring at the overhead lights. Sleep sounded to him at that moment. But then he remembered. He lifted his head and glanced at the wide-open exit, that he was supposed to secure.

"Fine, first door. Then sleep."

"How long has it been?" Violet asked no one in particular.

"About ten minutes. I think," said Ms. Kashatri.

"He should have been back by now." She knew she couldn't leave him out there, no matter what happened to him. She'd read about American military never leaving a man behind. She always thought that was a noble endeavor and vowed herself then to do the same for her people. "Mr. Akashi, I'm going out to check. Please secure this door behind me."

Violet stuck her head out the door; looking ahead, she saw him immediately. She pulled herself back in. "I'll need your help," Violet whispered now. "Ms. Kashatri, man the door."

She popped her head back out, checking in all directions. She whispered again, "Come with me" and darted out the door. Mr. Akashi followed.

Violet quickly saw that there were several dead bodies and their own Igor, who also looked dead, in a pool of blood. A large bloom of red covering most of his white shirt told her it was his. The door to the outside starboard exit was shut. She also heard someone coming up the stairs.

"We need to drag him back," she said, grabbing one of Ivanov's arms, Akashi grabbing the other.

In the process of lugging Igor Ivanov's giant frame across the floor, Violet could see he was still breathing, though barely.

They made it back inside their area and secured it, leaving a long trail of blood.

She had no idea if he'd survive, but she didn't leave anyone behind. Not today.

23

Coordinated Attack

The explosion sent Jay Falcone down onto his knees. Jay cocked his head all the way back and studied the ceiling, certain this was the explosion's origin and it would collapse on top of him.

Jay continued to gaze upward into the murk, just noticing there were only two small lights on in the whole theater. He couldn't remember if this was new, or if it had been the same the last time he'd done this.

The explosive tremors quickly subsided, but then they grew again. Now, the growing rumble and its accompanying noise—like the shuffling feet of hundreds—were coming not from above, but from the stage area. Jay turned his gaze to the growing tremors, wondering if this was the prelude to another explosion.

He had no idea how much worse it would be.

Only a few days ago, after a marathon day of poker, capped off by winning the ship's poker tournament, Jay celebrated with the Bucket of Beer special and an unfunny comedy show, featured on this very stage. This current performance was far more mesmerizing. And in response, Jay's mouth dropped open. His brain just couldn't accept what his eyes were hollering at it: a multitude of naked men and women were dashing across the stage.

Frozen in his place, Jay didn't budge even as the first of these naked performers, racing in his direction, touched down on the carpeted aisle. When they began to yell their torturous screams and they were close enough for him to see their red eyes, that's when Jay sprang.

Boom.

In his panicked dash, Jay caught just a glimpse of the guard's rifle crashing in front of him. Then beside him.

Boom-boom-boom!

Even in his youth, Jay was not much of a runner. Yet he'd already passed the guard, allowing his gaze to hang on the man one last second before he bounded out the door. Jay didn't dare look back any longer.

The guard—Jay had already forgotten his name—remained on a bent knee, discharging his rifle, now on automatic fire. In Jay's final glimpse, before turning to face the main entrance, he caught a white streak hit the guard so hard, it knocked him backwards.

Jay had just enough time to take in the faces of the two wide-eyed guards before they disappeared behind the closing doors—his only way out of this.

The realization hit him at the same time Jay felt something barrel into his back with the power of a freight train, sending him careening hard into three overturned seats. Coming to rest on his back, neck ratcheted up, he watched multiple blurs of white, brown and black whisk past his field of vision. His sensory world was awash with the banshee-like cries of these human-animals, their mind-numbing pounding on the door and then the face of one of these bare-skinned monsters.

At one time it was a woman, and a pretty one too, with its long red hair and attractive figure. Now this woman was the stuff of nightmares: it brayed at him, its mouth opened wide, its red eyes blazing absolute hatred. Without warning, it stuck its thumb into his left eye socket. Jay attempted to react, lifting a hand to protect his other eye, but she struck again with the force and speed of lightning.

His mind—since he had no eyes to see—filled with flashes of bright light and equally searing pain. All he could do now was scream his blind terror.

The she-beast did its best to silence him, but his escalating screams of panic and pain lasted the longest minute of his shortened life. He sensed its teeth, followed by many others, violently rip into his skin, all of them pulling and tearing at the flesh of his arms, legs and chest, until at long last, Jay felt nothing.

Then, like Jay, the lounge was plunged into darkness.

D r. Molly watched with dread as both an observant scientist and a feeling person.

Her eyes welled with tears, which she couldn't hold back when she saw the pain on the volunteer's face, as one of their parasitics viciously attacked him and literally ripped him apart.

The scientist in her marveled at the speed and agility of its assault, as well as its vindictive voracity to rob the man of his eyesight before it ate up his life. It was as if the parasitic was punishing him for gazing at its nakedness, even though Molly would have thought that parasitics no longer cared about these things: parasitics weren't burdened by such human frailties as pride, fear or empathy.

Molly had never seen this kind of action in the animal or parasitic kingdoms before: animals and parasites killed for food or to fulfill what they were genetically programmed to do. The only beings who killed for revenge or sport were humans. Molly was observing the worst of combinations: human anger and cunning, mixed with animalistic reflexes and strength.

The parasitic woman then appeared to call out to the others, as many joined her to pounce on the man, ripping at him and feeding on him, while he was obviously very much alive and screaming in pain.

She shuddered at this whole episode. These creatures were advancing in so many more ways that she could have guessed.

So riveted was she by what was unfolding, Molly was barely aware of Mr. Deep continuing to holler on his radio. He had finally connected with security and mechanical. But it would do no good. She knew after observing this attack that once this new species was free on their ship, they were all doomed. There was no place to hide, as these parasitics would eventually break down every door to get to their prey. They were as smart as humans, now coordinated, bloodthirsty and lacking all the human hang-ups. In short, they were the perfect killing machines and they would prevail over their human forebears. And there was nothing she or anyone else could do about it.

Molly felt gutted. Every muscle and bone in her old body cried out in physical and emotional agony. She just wanted to give up...

But they weren't.

She looked up from the big monitor, her watery eyes blurring the scene on one of the other monitors. Blinking away her sense of doom, she could see something was going on outside the lounge.

She scooched forward and sat up in her seat to see better.

At least my fellow humans are not giving up yet, she thought.

She always had hope in and a strong belief for what would come after this life ended. She'd just been losing hope in humans in this life. Ted said he had really believed in the human spirit. She hadn't been so sure anymore. And yet, here was her proof.

Security and volunteers from around the ship were arriving at the main entrance and the side door, to try and shore them up. They were all working together to try and save their ship and seemed to be holding back the horde.

The side door was their biggest problem. There was too much damage, caused by just two parasitics. Now there was an uncountable horde, pushing, pounding and beating the door down.

And yet Molly could see her fellow humans on the other side, trying to stab the parasitics with poles and she suspected, because they didn't have cameras back there, they were employing the same techniques that they were at the main entrance: heavy items and wedges. Was it even possible?

Then the four monitors on which they'd focused all their attention, went black.

Molly steepled her hands together and said a silent prayer, tuning out the horrific screaming coming from Deep's radio.

24

Last Stand

When Paulo Oliveira saw the stampeding horde of crazies overtake their people, he was sure they waited too long to shut the lounge doors. But somehow, they did, just as their non-human bodies struck the doors, one after another, delivering an inconceivable amount of pounding and shaking.

He and Jason Anderson, a new addition to his security team, took multiple steps back and watched the doors shudder and shake. They could feel the tremors below their feet and all around them. And it continued to build. When Paulo heard a cracking sound, he knew either he had to turn tail and run or do something before they broke through.

Then the lights went off and the entire area was plunged into darkness. The pounding continued unabated, though. When the emergency lights popped on, Paulo knew what he had to do.

"Help me," he barked at Anderson.

They grabbed a heavy coffee table, just outside the lounge entrance, and drove it hard into the door.

Others joined them, some from security and some from mechanical, all grabbing heavy pieces of furniture and moving them to the door.

"Wait! We need to wedge them," announced a slight man from mechanical, his grease-covered hands demonstrating. The man looked around the area for something, until he was jolted by a vision from another sitting area.

"Here. Help me now." The man grabbed Paulo's elbow and pulled him with him to another elaborate wood table with curved feet.

"You break. We use under door as wedge."

Paulo understood right away, nodding. He turned the heavy table on its side; the glass top slid off and broke into a hundred pieces, some long and lethal-looking. He searched for the weak point in the legs and drove his foot into that point, separating two legs at their joints. Pulling one away, he handed it to the small man from mechanical, who dashed to the door, then around the group of helpers pushing furniture toward the doors, stopping before the table Paulo and Anderson had just used to buttress one of the doors. Already two more were on top.

The small man stuck the curved wedge under the door and kicked it a couple of times. "One more," he yelled.

Paulo bashed the table into three curved wedge pieces and ran over to the small man, handing him one of the pieces. Paulo took another and used it like a hammer to pound the already set wedge in harder, while the little man set up the one he'd given him under the other door. Paulo pounded at that one as well.

"Thank you," Paulo announced with a smile.

The man didn't smile back; he stood up and said, "Come with me, need others." He grabbed the other pieces from Paulo. "Side door bad. Must fix before they break out." The small man grabbed a tool bag he must have left on the floor and ran to the crew access door at the far side of the hall.

"Stack up more furniture against here," Paulo yelled to the now twenty men and woman who had showed up to help, while pointing at the bottom of the doors. "Then, I need a dozen of you to wait here."

Paulo dashed back to where he had broken the tabletop and carefully picked up pieces of the thick broken glass. He pulled off his button-down work shirt and wrapped the pieces inside. In a quick dash back, he passed his dozen-plus volunteers and yelled, "Follow me."

Paulo didn't look back as he ran to the side entrance to the back of the lounge, used only by crew and performers. A thousand memories raced through his head as he opened it and held it for the others to follow.

A couple of years back, Paulo had an affair with one of the young performers. He had used this entrance to visit with her before and after her performances. And inside was one of the few places he knew where they could be intimate together and no one would know.

At the back of a dark hallway, barely illuminated by the single emergency bulb in the corner, was a storage closet. When he and Lucy had their affair, this room had just been cleaned out. Last he had seen, housekeeping used it for storage. He was counting on this.

Flicking on his Maglite, illuminating the door handle, he held the bundle of wrapped broken glass under an armpit and fished for his keys. Once open, he flashed his light inside. "Eureka," he said. He laid the broken-glass bundle down and entered the storage room.

Paulo came back out with several push brooms. "You," he said to one of his volunteers, "twist off the brooms from the handles."

Another trip back into the room and he came out with a pile of rags. "Okay, some space please." He plopped his pile next to his shirt bundle, which he opened. Snatching an extra-long piece of glass and a rag, he stood up straight.

"Okay, watch," he said while slicing the rag into three long pieces. He wrapped one of the pieces around the base of the long splinter of glass he was using as a knife. "You," he said to a woman nearest him, "make more long pieces like this out of these rags." He flipped the glass-knife around and handed it to her.

"Okay, I need a broom handle." Someone handed him one.

"Now," he reached into his shirt and grabbed another fragment. "We're going to make spears. Tie the glass like this to the ends of the broom handles. Do it now and then meet me in back."

Paulo then left them, holding his newly-made spear, hoping they'd follow his lead. He turned a corner and felt his hope die.

The small man was stabbing a crazy trying to get through the top of the broken door. It wedged its way through the opening at the top of the door and grabbed the small man and tossed him down, either knocking him out cold or killing him.

The crazy turned just as Paulo drove his spear into its eye socket. He pulled back and then kicked the naked crazy in the head with his boot, just for good measure.

He turned to face the door, as it was literally being pulled off its hinges.

Paulo jabbed with his spear, getting several.

Then others joined in, also jabbing and slashing with their own homemade spears.

The ship should have killed them all, rather than believing they could hold them. There was no holding back these beasts. He knew they'd eventually get through.

Even though Paulo's brain rapid-fired these thoughts, he felt no anger at his ship's officers for their ignorance. In fact, for some strange reason, he was filled with pride right then.

Rather than abandoning him, as he probably would have done after seeing their situation was so hopeless, one after another of his volunteers showed up with their homemade spears. They stood toe-to-toe with the beasts, stabbing and slashing at them, probably killing quite a few.

Never did his volunteers falter. They held until the very end, when the door came off and they were overwhelmed.

25

Jaga

Jaga was rattled awake. He gazed into the darkness, disoriented and just trying to get his bearings. His hand touched emptiness, where there should have been a table and his flashlight. This tool allowed him to quietly navigate his way in between his roommates' bunk beds to the bathroom door at the end of their cabin. Now, his table and flashlight were gone.

An ember of fright started to glow red in his gut.

Next, he turned to his left and felt around for Taufan, who often slept by his head, but his ferret wasn't there either. And the cabin wall that was always there was gone: the bed went on forever, as did emptiness above.

The smoldering coal of fright burst into a hot flame of alarm.

He swung his legs out of his sheets and onto the floor, his feet instantly sensing a supple carpet as opposed to the rubberized flooring that he was used to. The same rubberized flooring that his roommates constantly made a fuss about Asap not cleaning when it was his turn was gone. "Guys, are you there?"

Silence.

The fire of alarm in his belly now exploded into a wildfire of panic.

He heaved out breaths and took in short puffs of putrid air. Looking for some shred of recognition, he noticed a small shaft of light, cleaving its way from behind a curtain, where there shouldn't have been one. A flood of images dashed through his head: he was in a new cabin; he'd lain down on his new bed, relishing its softness; he must have fallen asleep, even though he didn't intend to; he didn't have any roommates anymore and he was split up from his best friend Yacobus; Catur was dead and Asap was a monster now.

He dashed over to the curtain, desperately wanting the light of reality to confirm that this wasn't just some nightmare, but then hesitated.

Do I really want reality or to fall back into a dream?

The curtains flew open, and a foggy beam lit his new cabin. The air inside had substance... *Smoke!*

A quick sniff only made him cough. It smelled a little like smoke, but also something else... *Dead fish?*

He looked for a vent, not remembering where it was in this room, his eyes now sore, like they were burning. He found it above the bathroom and scrutinized it for a second. Little wisps of white smoke leapt in from the register.

It was enough. Something was happening, and he only knew he had to get out.

Taufan!

"Taufan? Taufan, where are you buddy?" he yelled out, now feeling overwhelmed by a raging bonfire of panic. He had to find Taufan and get out now!

"Taufan, please, where are you?"

Jaga slipped on his sandals, glad that they were by the bed, right where he left them.

He padded over to the closet. There was no time to change out of his pajamas, but he'd put on his house coat if it was cool and because of its special pocket.

"Taufan," he pleaded, almost in tears. "Please, say something."

He froze.

Was it the squeak of his sandals on the carpet or did he hear his little buddy?

Squeak-squeak-squeak.

Jaga heard the muffled cries coming from the closet. He flicked on the light switch, but nothing happened—-*the power was off.* He tossed open the bi-fold glass door way too hard, and Taufan shot out, hopping once on the carpet, and bounded into his arms. He barked once and then gave out a slow whine; his body shivered. Jaga kissed his head, but took no time to relish this moment.

"We need to get out of here, Taufan," Jaga announced, as he held him with one hand and rifled through his canvas duffel bag in the back of the closet. He had thrown it there when he arrived.

Of course his robe was near the bottom.

Upon grabbing it, Jaga slipped one arm inside and then moved Taufan to his other hand and slipped in the other arm.

"Okay, my friend. Time for a ride," he coaxed, holding Taufan over the giant-sized pocket. He had sewed this into this house coat so he could carry his ferret around with him, without anyone knowing he was there.

Taufan hopped in, still whining.

The air in his cabin was getting very stale and hard to breathe. But he needed something more.

Jaga held a sleeve over his mouth and searched the cabin once again, until he found it.

A quick shuffle to his table, which was lower than his previous table and probably why his hand couldn't find it. Right in the center was his large black Maglite, a gift from a passenger some years ago, and his sea card. He snatched the heavy flashlight, thinking he might need it if there was a fire, and then shuffled back to the door.

Just before opening, he heard voices. Lots of them.

A swarm of people were just outside his door, milling around and speaking to each other in short agitated sentences.

"Jaga, hello," called out a familiar voice from the crowd, which he recognized as a mix of passengers and crew. *Or should that be new crew and old crew?*

It was Samuel Yusif, from Somalia. He didn't bump into Samuel much, because he worked in the kitchen, but he liked him. "Hey Samuel, is there a fire?" Jaga jammed the Maglite in between the door and frame, now wondering why he didn't grab his sea card too. He stood up again to find Samuel there.

"We just trying to figure this out ourselves too. Dis smell like burned garlic... After de explosion, we see gas in cabins. Come out here. That when—"

"Explosion? What explosion?"

"Some say it bomb."

Jaga was puzzled by this, now realizing that the explosion must have been what woke him. "Hey look, the smoke is coming into the hallway." Jaga pointed to a vent in the hall. The same white smoke was wafting out of the vent, but not like a regular fire. This was something else, like a gas.

"It's poison," someone yelled out.

"Maybe," Jaga hollered over the din of harried conversations, "we should get into the stairwell. The ventilation is best there. And if we have to, we can run down stairs and away from the gas or smoke, if it isn't safe." He wasn't about to call it poison, just because someone said this. But he wondered if it was.

His words were having an effect, because the people in his hallway were already moving down the hall and turning into the stairwell.

"Aren't you coming?" Samuel asked, following the group.

Jaga glanced at his door, propped open slightly by his flashlight. He was going to grab his sea card, but now he was having second thoughts. If this was a poisonous gas, the last thing he wanted to do is breathe any more of it. And right now his skin and throat felt prickly, like they were burnt. *Probably just my mind playing tricks on me, but just in case...* He snatched the flashlight from the door, which instantly clasped shut. He'd get another card, or ask someone to let him in again, if given that chance. "I'm coming."

The group of ten or so people, now his neighbors, had already filed into the landing area in between the midway elevators and stairwell. He quickly followed, anxious to get away from the poisonous gas that was slowly leaking into their cabins and hallway.

"I'm so glad you here, Jaga," Samuel stated. "Now what we do?"

The others cut off their conversations and looked to him. He found this odd, because other than a few friends, people rarely found what he had to say interesting, much less important.

"I think we wait here. The gas doesn't seem to be moving fast, and I'm guessing that's because the power outage and probably the explosion automatically closed the vents. We have good ventilation here. So I would suggest we wait for the captain or crew to instruct us and we listen."

So they quietly waited. But rather than an expected announcement, they heard something strange above them.

"Do you hear that?" someone whispered.

It was like animals... Hundreds of breathless animals, in a stampede.

26

Engine Room

The experienced engine room crew calmly followed protocol immediately upon feeling the explosion rock the ship, even before they received any confirmation from their engineering chief. In anticipation of a gas explosion or even a terrorist attack, they attempted to do what they were supposed to do first: secure all doors. The automatic systems took care of the rest. The protocol and automated systems were designed to lower the possibility of a fire spreading and/or cut off any access terrorists might have to their engines. However, many of the new and inexperienced crew members did the opposite. They panicked.

Bobby Gibson, a retired banker from Cheltenham, ran as fast as he could for the nearest exit, which thankfully was right in front of him. When his new supervisor, Edger Ivonovich, had abandoned him to follow some sort of "emergency protocol," Bobby figured he'd take his chances topside. He'd get out of here and face the consequences later.

At the small steel door, there was a placard that read "Deck 1" with an up arrow. That's all Bobby needed. He heaved up on the metal handle until it budged, slowly at first, then finally sliding all the way up with a large clank. He pulled on the same metal latch to open the door, but it was stuck. So he yanked at it with all of his might, and then tugged again, until something in the door and in his back gave way with a loud *thunk* sound. He held onto the latch, while taking in several rapid puffs of air. Besides whatever he pulled in his back, his chest was beating so fast now, he thought it might explode.

A noise behind him caused him to turn back. He didn't see them, but he could hear frantic voices coming toward him. *Need to move quickly.*

Another tug at the door caused it to swing open. Without hesitating, he stepped blindly into a soupy fog on the other side. His skin burned immediately, as the fog—or was it smoke—surrounded him. *If there's smoke, there's fire,* he thought. Yet this smelled like melting fish guts. Something was wrong here and he had to find another way out of the engine room.

Bobby took a quick turn, attempting to return to the way he had entered. He took one step and he ran into something solid; a pin-prick of pain shot through his forehead. He couldn't see a damned thing in this smoke and his eyes were on fire. So were his lungs. He took another breath and coughed hard.

Now really panicking, he spun farther left on his heel, thinking he had turned prematurely, took another step and this time ran face-first directly into a sharp but equally solid object. Bobby lost it at that point.

"Help me!" he screamed.

Gagging on the smoke, he thrust out his hands and desperately tried to feel his way to the opening. Every square inch of his skin felt on fire. "Hell—cough-cough, plea—cough-cough."

He found the opening, thrusting his two arms out to confirm it, and then dashed for it. This time he forgot to lift his feet over the threshold of the bulkhead door, designed to be air and water-tight. His feet remained inside the access way, but his body continued moving forward, until he hit head-first on the grated walkway. Bobby no longer felt panic, nor the sting of the toxic gas.

As he slowly died, the toxic gas, finding its release, billowed inside the engine room, filling it up fast.

F lavio dispatched another one of the island men. This one was loitering by the main entrance of the engine room. At first he was going to shoot him with his rifle. Quick and easy. But he opted for a more silent method and withdrew his Morakniv.

Flavio surprised the man and before he could react, Flavio sliced across the man's neck and then drove his knife down, deep into the man's chest, at the same time shoving with all of his weight to knock the man onto his back. The man did what all do: he clutched his hands around his neck to hold back the flow of blood. With one gloved hand still on the knife stuck in the man's chest, Flavio placed the other over the man's mouth to keep him quiet, while Flavio waited for him to die and searched for the others.

It took less than a minute for his target to stop moving. There was no one else around.

Glancing back down at the dead man, Flavio was momentarily jolted. The man's eyes were blood-red. They were just like Mrs. Williams' eyes. That meant that his man was symptomatic like her.

He hesitated before extracting his knife, wiping the blood off it onto the symptomatic's chest. Immediately, he felt a sigh of relief. He probably couldn't win a hand-to-hand battle with one of these things. Mrs. Williams could certainly kick his ass if she tried. And certainly any somewhat able-bodied man with double or triple their normal strength would be a difficult force to stop. Worse would be several of them at once.

No more stealth, he reasoned, sliding his knife back in its sheath attached to his belt. He left his small pack by the door, stood up and brought his rifle back around, at the ready. He flicked off the safety, did another scan of his surroundings, and then clicked open the main entrance door to the engine room.

His gun was thrust inside, but he held up there, listening. The fluorescents above revealed a misty wasteland. Some sort of fog held to the floor, covering four or five bodies. One wore a black jumper like he'd expect of the crew that worked here. His head looked bashed in and his throat looked ripped out. This told Flavio that more of these island men were symptomatic or parasitic. He wondered if the two men they had confronted in the food area were as well, even though Mrs. Williams said they were not. But she also said something was wrong with them.

As the fog started to inch its way out the door, surrounding his boots, Flavio scrutinized the other bodies. They were the island men, wearing the same dirty clothes and sunglasses—*many of them had sunglasses, just like Williams, to hide their eyes.* He could only see two of them clearly. Their faces were covered in red sores and their mouths were wide open, like they had suffocated. Their throats were swollen to twice their normal size.

The fog crept up his knee. And that was close enough. He withdrew his rifle from the opening and stepped back, quickly shutting the door and closing off the gas.

He had seen this stuff used before, to kill rats as well as people. He hesitated, thinking about what would happen if someone else happened to open the door. Whoever was in the engine room was probably dead already, or would be soon, and it wasn't worth risking any others. He flipped his rifle around to his back and undid his leather belt.

It took only a minute to tie up the handle of the door, just enough so that no one would accidentally stumble inside.

He then left the engine room, with the intent of going to try and help TJ with the men targeting the bridge. Even as talented as she was, she'd still need help.

While running, he reported the probable death of all of the engine room crew and the island men who were trying to target that area. He also announced his intent to help Mrs. Williams and that some of the islanders were symptomatic.

Flavio made it to the deck 2 landing, telling Mr. Williams that he intended to ascend the stairwell all the way to deck 8 and then forward to the bridge.

"Flavio, don't go that way," Williams warned. "The parasitics are breaking free directly above you. Suggest instead you—" Flavio clicked off the radio.

Right above him were the sounds of many people—he now suspected the parasitics—coming down these stairs, and they were less than a deck away.

27

TJ

After hearing and feeling the explosion, TJ wasn't sure what to expect. The words of the disgusting Squat man rattled in her brain: "While you're feeling me out, my men are taking over your bridge and will blow your engines so you can't go anywhere." In addition to the perversity of this man, the sheer temerity of these people to come on board and believe they could do what they wanted to her people, pissed her off to no end.

TJ was ready to kill and she didn't care what the repercussions were. She was done holding back, repressing her desire to kill. These men needed to die in the most gruesome ways and she was going to enjoy every moment of it. Then she was going to come back to where they were holding Squat and pop his head like a pimple.

Her smile grew, as did her stride, as she turned off of I-95, hoping this shortcut would get her to the bridge before the islanders did, or at least before they were able to take out the bridge door.

She turned into the extra-dark crew stairwell, barely lit by emergency lights. She punched through the murky area, ascending three steps at a time, and was on deck 8 in barely a blink or two. It was almost frightening how quickly she could move now. At the top step, she froze and came to an abrupt stop.

Before her was a man dressed just like Squat and Skinny: a sheen of dirt, grime and sweat coated his skin, face and clothes. This one had a broken ankle; his foot was bent at a ninety-degree angle. He sat on the decking, legs splayed, making a meal out of someone's arm.

The man looked up, glared at TJ with his red eyes and brayed a series of cackles at her. TJ instantly knew that this meant, "Stay away, this is mine."

Below his elbow, in puddles of blood and muck were his sunglasses. *Some wore sunglasses and some were wearing black contacts,* she reasoned.

But why no smell?

But there was a smell; in between the non-infected blood, she could smell it.

She pulled out the knife Flavio had given her from the fold of her shorts and thrust it into the ear of the dirty parasitic. His head flopped over and the half-eaten arm he'd been munching on, tumbled to the floor. With her other hand, TJ wiped the sheen of dirt and sweat from the man's face and smelled it, and then him.

Also remembering something she saw in Squat, she pushed the dead man's head back and glared into his nostrils, which were flared like the others'.

Then she understood immediately: The nostrils were filled with cotton so they couldn't smell. Their own smell was someone else's dirt and sweat. They were using a non-infected's body odor and dirt to cover the island's infected. These men were infected and symptomatic like her, although some like this one, looked parasitic, all to overtake their ship. And so they wouldn't go crazy until they needed them to, they shoved cotton up their noses, so they couldn't smell their own scent masks.

"Those..." So many expletives rapid-fired out of her brain at that moment, they got stove-piped at her tongue and wouldn't come out. She stepped forward, crunching the dead man's sunglasses under her feet, turned the handle and threw back the door, not caring whether she was stealthy or not.

She was going to wreak havoc upon these men.

TJ leapt into the hallway and ran around the public stairway to take the starboard hallway toward the bridge.

She turned the corner, past the entrance of Eloise Carmichael's cabin, and dashed toward the men already there and setting up explosives at the bridge entrance.

One of the men's radio was hollering at him and he picked it up to answer it, when he saw TJ. The man dropped his radio and stared at the beautiful blur coming right at him. His lips attempted to form words, but all that fell out was, "Look at—" before TJ struck him like a wrecking ball, crashing him hard into cabin 8000's doorframe.

TJ was able to stop right where she'd struck him, sparing herself from a potentially concussive blow. But something hit her as strongly as the man she'd run into, who now writhed in pain on the floor. The man was not infected. And that meant that only some of their group were infected and others weren't. This was puzzling.

It was a flash of movement, just out of her periphery. She snapped her head in that direction. There, a few feet from her, was a smiling face, pointing a revolver; the revolver's chambers were filled with .357 cartridges; it clicked. Before she could react, the smiling face pulled the trigger.

28

Tomas

Tomas Novo, Via de Corvo's only surviving agent, listened patiently to his boss ranting on the radio.

"Team A. Team B. Report goddammit, report!" Sal hollered, spewing spittle and anger at the radio. Not getting a response, he was naturally inspired to take action, as he always did. He pulled back, portable in his palm. Then, because he got no response, he smashed the radio against the rough stonework of the building they were in. The radio splintered into a multitude of now useless pieces. Sal glared at the cruise ship out the window and then at the broken parts of what was his radio.

Tomas sat quietly behind his boss, unwilling to offer even one thought or suggestion. He'd wait until he was asked. And he certainly didn't want to venture a guess now, when he was so mad. When Sal got mad, people died. And Sal was as angry as Tomas had seen him in several days.

It was a common theme with his boss: he'd lose his temper and then break something, or someone. Only then was he able to collect his logical thoughts and refocus on the task at hand.

Tomas knew enough to let him be and wait for the anger to pass and his logic to return. Until then, he didn't make a peep.

"Tomas? Hand me your radio."

Tomas popped out of his seat and took the few steps to Sal. He laid it down on the table between Sal and the window, through which he still stared at the elusive object that had been avoiding his capture. That was the root of his anger, not being able to easily seize the *Intrepid*, even though he had thought it would be so easy; even though he had made all the plans he made. He just couldn't wait to get his hands on it and enough food to supply his people for at least a year or two.

Tomas quickly pulled back and returned to his chair.

Sal picked up the radio and studied it, like it was some sort of puzzle box he wasn't sure how to open.

This often happened after his explosion of anger. He'd almost get delirious with anger and then confused afterwards.

"Why?" Sal paused, as if he wasn't sure what words to add to the end of the sentence. Though Tomas was pretty sure what the question was: "Why don't... they answer?"

This is where Tomas had to be extra careful.

He'd seen this very thing happen with the other agent, maybe two days after the barge crashed into their island. Sal went on an anger bender, smashing a car with a cricket bat, all because he couldn't find the keys, which it turned out he left in his desk in the station.

After ten minutes of Sal assaulting the car with the cricket bat, the other agent, went inside, grabbed Sal's keys and came back out to offer them to him. When Sal stopped his tirade and just stared blankly at the car for an untold amount of time, he finally said, "I wonder where I put my keys."

The other agent said, "I've got 'em right here, sir," jingling them like a trophy.

Sal looked at the keys and then the agent, and then proceeded to beat him to death with the cricket bat.

Tomas and the others in town knew then that Salvadore Calderon had become mentally unstable and a psychopath.

From this incident and other people's trial and error, Tomas learned to give an answer that sounded logical, but wasn't complete either. The combination seemed to force Sal to think more about it. This, for some reason, reconnected his logical thoughts and brought him back to someone Tomas could deal with.

Sal had sent in two teams so far. Team A was supposed to go to the bridge, blow the door, and take the captain hostage for later torture. Team B was to blow the ship's engine—Tomas never told Sal that there were two engines—and thus disable the ship, so it would have to remain at their dock permanently. Then they'd take over the ship and take its food, as they wanted.

Neither team had reported on their radios, which they were supposed to do after they blew their explosives and completed their missions. They heard one explosion. But nothing since.

"Maybe," Tomas offered, "the teams are trying to be quiet and not alert the *Intrepid's* people as to where they are."

Sal stood almost completely unmoving, other than his breaths. Then he turned to Tomas and said, "Okay, it's time to send in Team Z now!"

At first, Tomas thought maybe Sal wanted him to take his radio back and call in the order, but then Sal did this himself. "Team C, send in Team Z. Make sure they have taken down the ship before entering."

This part was disheartening, even though Tomas knew where this was going. Tomas somehow hoped he was wrong about Sal, even though he knew better.

It was just that, as insane as this man was, he still in a sick way cared for him like a father. And he knew that Sal cared for Tomas like a son. It was the real reason why Tomas had, in fact, never been seriously threatened by Sal. Even though Sal did threaten him with death or dismemberment, and did so to so many others, Tomas never really believed it.

He went along with Sal all this time, always hoping that he wasn't really going to kill all these people. But when he called for Team Z, as in the last group from A to Z: the final solution, Tomas knew the die was cast. There was no going back.

As he listened, three of Sal's four men who were Team C, opened the doors of the three shipping containers—hidden in plain sight, behind them on the dock. Then the fourth member of Team C blasted a horn on the other end of the dock. That was the signal.

The mob of people, some thirty men and woman, stampeded out of the three shipping containers and raced down the dock with one intent: kill everyone on the *Intrepid*.

Tomas saw them race by the little building they were in, yelling their battle cry, and Tomas lowered his head.

He couldn't do anything about this, but he could do something about his boss. He knew right then what he would do next, and when.

"Come on, my son. It's time for the last part of my plan. You and I are up."

29

Flavio

At first, Flavio pointed his rifle up the stairs, but then he second-guessed himself: if there were hundreds of parasitics pouring down the stairs, he didn't have enough ammo. He spun around, looking for a way out, and saw only the starboard gangway area was open; he'd have to get the door closed... They were already here. He spun back, flicked his rifle to full auto and readied himself. Their feet were visible in between the steps and then he saw them, when they hit the mid-deck landing.

He clicked the safety back on.

It was just a bunch of scared people. That's all.

He recognized the leader of the group as Jaga, who recognized him as well.

"They're coming." Jaga jumped the last step, then moved to his left. "The crazies are above us." Jaga was headed down to deck 1 next.

Flavio had an idea.

"No. Go there." He pointed to the starboard gangway area. "Slide interior door closed and be quiet. Go now!"

Flavio didn't even wait for them, he sprinted to the port-side interior door, which led to the exit his security had secured. Before pounding on it, he eyeballed the fresh blood streak leading inside and wondered if they were all right. "It's Flavio Petrovich... Ah, Second Officer Petrovich. You there?"

Flavio could hear the rumble above, coming down the stairs, while the dozen or so friends of Jaga were making their way to the starboard exit area, albeit much too slowly.

The door slid open. "Hello, sir," said Violet Johansson.

He wanted to ask them about the blood streak, but there was no time. "Open interior wall and hide. Then when I tell you, open exit door."

"But the islanders... They're on the other side." Johansson shot him a look of curious fear.

Flavio could hear them pounding on the other side of the metal hatch. This made his plan even better.

"Trust me. This work for everybody. Open exactly when I say, but everyone must hide now or you die."

She nodded.

He took a few steps toward the starboard exit, just outside the port-side hallway. Doing a quick check, he could see Jaga's group was having difficulty sliding the interior wall closed. As he laid his rifle down, he looked back to the port side. They were pushing their wall open, but not fast enough. "Hurry!" he yelled to both sides.

Above, he heard a collection of animalistic grunts and fervent barks and the shuffling of a multitude of feet. They were close and moving fast.

Flavio needed to get ready.

He lowered his pack and withdrew an air-horn. He thought he might have a need for this and was right.

They were right above him now.

Johansson had the port side ready. They were hidden and Flavio could see her hand on the control pad button that would open the hatch. The pounding from the other side seemed to get louder.

When he looked starboard, he was shocked to see their wall was still half open, with Jaga and another tugging, until one lost his footing and fell to the floor.

They were sitting ducks.

He stabbed the switch on the compressed air can with this thumb, sending it through the horn, causing it to emit a horrendously loud blare. Then he released his thumb. "Come and get some fine Romanian meat," Flavio yelled.

The stampede swung into his view, but stopped at the mid-deck landing. A horde of parasitics filled the stairs leading up and out of sight. In front of the horde was Ágúst Helguson, his pale face highlighted by a ring of red around his mouth. Helguson glanced at Flavio, who just glared back at him. Helguson turned to his right and saw all the people trying to hide in the semi-open area.

The horde of parasitics behind him were like an enormous pack of mad pit-bulls, snarling their anticipation at taking a bite out of a neighbor that'd been bothering them. All appeared to be held back by Helguson, as if they were waiting for his command.

Jaga and his people were easy pickings and so was Flavio, but he was just one person. The target was obvious.

Helguson turned back to Flavio, a grin slowly formed on his red-rimmed mug. He then abruptly pointed at Flavio and barked like a seal.

That was his cue.

Flavio had a long piece of duct tape fastened to the side of the airhorn. He pulled one side of the duct tape across the top and fastened it to the other side so that it put pressure on the button. The air-horn blared again while Flavio bolted to the port-side exit. "Now. Open door!" he hollered at the top of his lungs.

Johansson must have heard him because the port-side gangway exit slid open, revealing a mob of people, who all looked crazed themselves.

Flavio ran right at them holding his blaring airhorn up—the condensed air canister was cold as ice now.

The mob held at the door, even though they had easy access, apparently completely thrown off by Flavio's actions and the loud horn. Then they saw the hordes of parasitics flooding their way.

Flavio tossed the airhorn over the mob, past the gangway and onto the dock, where it bounced once before coming to rest, still blaring its call to all parasitics. Flavio leapt toward the mob, which had already course-corrected and was running the other way, no doubt because of the horde less than two seconds behind them.

Flavio felt a little like a gymnast as he nailed his jump, sailed above the gangway bridge railing and disappeared over the side of the boat, out of sight. While soaring, he reached back and just barely snagged the protective netting used to keep passengers from falling overboard. He clanged hard against the side of their ship, just above the water line.

30

TJ

The bullet had sliced through her cheek and scratched her cheekbone, but she didn't even feel it. She only knew it and reacted.

What happened next required no calculation; it was entirely impulse that moved TJ to spin on a heel and fling herself around.

The second bullet went way wide.

The smiling man attempted to correct on his third shot, while he squeezed the trigger, but she was much quicker, with her left wrist blocking his gun away and her right hand simultaneously slicing with her borrowed Morakniv—she didn't even remember unsheathing it—connecting a blood line from the man's cheek, down his neck and ending at his chest. In a blur, the knife was pushed back the other way and buried deep into the exposed side of the man.

As he tumbled to the floor, something inside TJ snapped. A stream of blood sprang from her cheek, rolled down her neck and covered her shoulder, but she still didn't feel her injury.

At that moment, she had clarity of purpose. Her anger past the boiling point, but there was so much more to it than anger. She had only one thing that mattered at that moment and nothing in this world could dissuade her: she was going to murder the other four men.

As if she stepped away from her conscious self, no longer an active participant in what happened next, she sliced and punched and kicked and bit at these men. As much as she was insane with madness, she was also filled with a strange calmness that warmed her whole body like an internal radiator.

Stoking this fire was an unquenchable hunger that wanted it all. Until this moment, she had tried so hard to repress this desire, but she gave into it now. And even though she could smell and taste that some of these men were infected like her, she didn't care. She indulged in their warm blood and the gore, as she ripped and tore and at one point, dismembered her enemies.

In barely the time it took to pull in a breath, there was only one standing: the one she first ran into. His whimpering cries sounded like a call to her and she wanted him even more because of it. Clutching his broken chest and limping slowly on a shattered leg, he didn't get far, tripping toward the floor. She bolted so fast to him, she caught him before he hit the floor, while at the same time, slicing her knife across his neck in one fluid motion, severing his carotid and most of his windpipe. It was better treatment than he deserved.

She held his shuddering body, his brown eyes fading and artery spurting a fountain of blood onto her face and into her mouth.

Ohhh, the taste.

She saw two more appear, while she licked her lips and drank down some of the man's life. She let him drop to the floor, while fixing her sights on these two, who looked familiar.

One called to her, as if to taunt her.

She'd take the bait.

When Ted heard the gun shot, knowing that his wife TJ was coming to the bridge, he was worried. With Wasano carrying his rifle behind him, Ted pushed open the door just as a blood-soaked TJ removed herself from a body in front of them, to race starboard down a hall to attack another.

Her speed was mesmerizing, grabbing the man before he fell from his nasty compound fracture. But it wasn't to save him. It was to drain the life out of him.

He watched her in disgust, as she sliced open the man's neck and even gulped at the spray of his blood.

Ted couldn't believe this was his wife. She looked like a wild animal who wore a coat of other people's blood.

It was even more eerie when she fixed her wild eyes on them.

"TJ, can you hear me? TJ, it's all right, honey."

Her eyes blinked from Wasano to Ted, to Wasano and back. Then she was focused on just Ted.

She looked like she might attack him.

Ted felt movement beside him and saw that Wasano was a foot away, lifting his rifle and pointing it directly at her.

She let the dead man drop at her feet, his blood coating her face, rivulets of red ran off her chin. Her mouth dropped open, as if she were about to say something. Her red eyes glared like two bullet-points, focused by the whites of her sclera, both drilling into him like a target. This was no longer his wife.

Wasano flipped off the safety. She darted forward. Wasano fired.

31

Eloise

Freedom was the simple goal she had had for her people and they had just achieved this now that they had broken out of their confined area. And in their pre-programmed exuberance to follow sound, her people had gone even farther, or Ágúst had led them farther.

Eloise was the last of her people to leave the ship. All the others had unwittingly followed the loud horn-noise, leading them off the ship to another group of humans. She had wanted them to leave the ship anyway, but only after they had killed and fed on the crew. Finding the island was just a bonus. Being on a large island would mean greater opportunities for feeding, where all their feeding opportunities were very limited on this ship.

As she approached the port-side gangway, she couldn't help but revel in what she saw before her.

Even the heavens above grew angrier by the minute. A clattering echo of thunder warned the world below—her world now—of the next stage of their continuing wrath.

The dock below was filled with her people, now ravaging the humans outside, after having escaped from their human captors on this ship. This island was now their island.

Standing at the edge of the gangway, she felt a sense of pride in her people.

But something is wrong, she thought.

The smells were wrong.

Beyond the gangway bridge, she noticed maybe twenty-five or more who weren't her people out on the dock, but they didn't smell like humans. In fact she couldn't smell any humans outside now, when she had approached this exit. Not one human. And she should be able to smell many humans, even in the distance, if this island were big.

The falling rain made it more difficult for her to catch the scent of humans.

And then she did.

Just then she got a whiff of strong human scents, but they weren't coming from outside.

She spun around to face the ship's interior and sniffed again. *The human scents are here, in this room,* she thought.

Her head snapped back to take in the air from this direct area, now catching more of it. There was more than one in here, but she couldn't see them. She screwed her eyes to any detail that would point her to them. Then she saw the human blood—she could smell this as well. A trail of red that began at the stairwell landing, stretched through the hallway, through this area and then led to a curtain on her right. Just then the curtain moved.

Knowing they were there, she should be able to hear them, hiding behind there. *As if they could hide from me,* she boasted to herself. But with the loud noises outside, she couldn't hear anything in this room. When her surroundings were quiet, she could hear their heartbeats.

But she did hear something and spun to her left. There she saw a human's hands clinging to the ship, just outside the opening. And another one, hiding just inside the door, behind the controls for the door.

Then she knew.

This was a trap.

And where was Ágúst? He should be here, with her. She selected him and told him what to do after he had become. She gave herself to him. She rarely did that when she was a mere human.

She turned back to her people, who weren't as enraged as before, because the horn-noise had stopped. They had ceased fighting with the others from the island, because they were all of the same kind.

But Ágúst was not anywhere to be seen.

She called out for him, bellowing a long, guttural grunt.

Her people and the island people looked up at her and regarded her cries.

Then she heard him. Ágúst was not outside with her people; he was still inside.

Ágúst couldn't explain any of it, but he knew this was right.

He had pointed them in the direction of the trap, sensing what the human called Flavio was trying to do. He was trying to lead them off the ship, even though Eloise's instructions were for them to take over the ship and kill the rest of the humans. But he couldn't let that happen.

Ágúst had thought he had lost his human self when he had consumed their flesh and gave himself to her. But when they had broken free and he was leading their people, killing anyone and everyone that was in their way, he understood that he still had a choice. And he chose his humanity, even though so little of it remained.

When they were following the group of humans down the stairs and came upon Flavio, he realized that all of those people they were following were infected too. Flavio wasn't infected, and he was leading them in.

And so he had chosen to send his people off the ship and save the humans and give them a chance at survival. And when they took the bait and left the ship, he was happy. He didn't even know he had that feeling still.

And so he hid with the small group of infected crew, on the other side, and watched them all leave.

But Eloise stopped.

She was too smart for their simple tricks, even if the rest weren't. And as he watched her consider their trap, he knew that she knew. And he knew she could smell them there, hiding from her.

It was when she called out to him that Ágúst knew what he had to do.

He stepped from the shadows and made his way to her, while her back was still to him and she was facing outside. When she called for him, he responded with his call in their language that he knew she would understand. He told her, "I've been here the whole time."

She spun around quickly to see him, her glare questioning. Unsure.

That's when he used his newfound speed and bolted for her.

She saw him, but didn't really know what he was doing until it was too late.

When he hit, he wrapped his arms around her and drove her out of the ship, onto the gangway bridge, where they both rolled down it, entangled in each other.

While he had a chance, knowing that she would kill him for this, he looked back and saw Flavio climbing back up into the ship.

"Close up, now!" Ágúst bellowed.

Ágúst caught a knowing grin from Flavio, who understood his sacrifice. But it didn't feel like a sacrifice. It was just the right thing to do.

As Eloise wiggled free from him, he watched the door to the ship shut them out.

He turned back to face Eloise and his fate, which he knew would come as quickly as her vengeance.

As a mere human, he was always afraid of death and everything else that was a part of him being human. He wasn't now.

He faced his death, remembering his life as a human and how he saved his ship.

32

Tomas

The cold drizzle quickly grew into a driving rain which pelted the windows so hard, Tomas feared they might break. He wasn't much of a ship's captain, having piloted the P114 only one other time, after his boss gave him a crash course on its operations. Trying to keep an eye on where he was going, he looked all around for the windshield wipers and couldn't find them. Then Sal's hand appeared silently from behind him, making him jump.

"It's right here," Sal stated, twisting a knob on the console that sent the blades slashing back and forth violently.

They rounded the stern of the *Intrepid*, now getting the full view of the giant cruise ship.

"You seem jumpy. No need to be. We'll succeed, just as planned." Sal's voice was smooth and in control now, not at all like he was earlier. This was also the time when he was most aware of everyone around him.

Tomas also knew his boss was spewing bluster. Sal had expected to be in complete control of the cruise ship by now. But somehow the ship's crew had thwarted Sal's every move. They weren't even supposed get any fuel from the barge, which was only a ruse to allow their armed crew on board, or what Sal called his version of a Trojan horse.

But that obviously didn't work either.

Tomas was pretty sure it was just Sal's way of being vindictive when he sent all of his crazy people to board the ship, with the idea that they'd kill everyone in sight. Not only were they not able to board the ship, but in addition to the thirty-plus crazy people on their island, the ship dumped over one hundred more on them. They were already running out of food for their current crazy residents, as they were down to only a few uninfected humans. That's why they needed this cruise ship.

"**Y**ou little people can't win. We're superior to you," snarled Squat, his reddish eyes bouncing from Flavio to TJ. "You know what I'm saying, honey. Right?" he grinned at TJ when he said this.

It was just reflexive recoil when TJ socked him with her balled-up fist. A smile crept up her face, though she tried to hold it back, so that she wouldn't pop the new stitches in her cheek. She rather enjoyed this, desperately wanting to put on a world of hurt on this dirty, sneering perverted man, who happened to be a symptomatic like her.

Squat attempted to wiggle his hands and legs free from his tightened table restraints. His head was strapped down as well, an extra measure by Flavio, not trusting the thick straps to completely hold the monster down.

They were tasked by the captain to get information from this man they called Squat, and to do so 'by any means.'

'Any means' gave her a lot of latitude in the interrogation and she planned to take full advantage of this order.

"You're wasting your time. You know I don't feel pain. And at some point I'll find a way to get free. Then I'll kill and eat each of you. But you..." again he turned to TJ, "I'll lick you first, before I—"

TJ struck him in the Adam's apple, her hand stiff like a chopping knife.

A spate of uncontrollable coughing erupted from Squat.

TJ let her smile curl up high, feeling the tug of her stitches reach their limit, while readjusting her crutch under the other armpit.

"Just tell us why you wanted our ship and our food. We have little raw meat and that's what you eat, right? And why hurt engines?" Flavio asked, scrutinizing the small, bulbous man with the deep-set scar in his mug.

"You..." Squat was trying to say something, but then burst out into a fit of laughter and coughing.

"This get us nowhere," bellowed Flavio. "Answer questions or I just kill you myself."

"You people really are"—he cleared his throat—"stupid, aren't you? You said it yourself. We only eat raw meat."

Once again, he leered at TJ, his tongue sticking out slightly. "Aside from this tasty one, I was going to have the pick of any of your passengers. And with three thousand, we weren't going to go hungry for a long time. And you brought your own food. We just couldn't believe our luck when you showed up. It was like a farmer bringing us fresh farm animals and the animals agreed to fatten themselves up with their own food. You were so gullible to think that we would give you fuel for just a little fo—"

TJ had had enough. This time, with her free hand, she struck him with a heavy metal tray she'd found on the table next to them, almost falling over in the process.

Tomas had pretended not to know Sal's real plans, mostly to protect himself. He figured if Sal cared enough not to let him know that they were planning to eat everyone lured to their island, he must want him around for a while.

But it had gone too far and he was just tired of being scared all the time. He lived in constant fear of his boss' anger or one of his boss' lieutenants or of one of the crazies, who he knew wanted to kill him and tear him apart. He was done accepting his fate.

When this cruise ship thwarted their actions, he thought there might be a chance, a way for him to stop this monster and for him to get off this island and go someplace safe.

He shuddered in anticipation.

"You're shivering. You should have brought a jacket," Sal said, his attention mostly on the *Intrepid* off their port side.

"All right, hold up there." Sal pointed to a spot on the starboard side of the *Intrepid's* bridge. "Guess I don't need these things." He pulled off his sunglasses and tossed them onto the small table beside Tomas. Sal flashed his dark red eyes at him. "I'm going to make our demands known," Sal said, snatching a bullhorn from a rack before punching open the door of their little bridge.

A swirl of rainwater poured in and then the door slammed shut.

Tomas watched his boss splash his way to their weapon on their boat's forecastle, all loaded and ready. Sal turned back to Tomas and held up his palm, indicating he wanted to stop here.

Tomas pulled the boat's throttle all the way back, causing them to slow to a couple of knots. He reversed the engines to halt their drafting, when he heard his boss's voice over the bullhorn.

"Ahoy there, Captain Jean Pierre Haddock of the *Intrepid*. This is Salvadore Calderon. We met a short time ago. Apparently I didn't make my demands clear; instead I attempted subterfuge, when clearly I'm dealing with an intelligent man. So I'll make myself perfectly clear now and I'm only going to say this once, so you better be listening, Captain Haddock of the *Intrepid*. You are to surrender your ship in the next two minutes or I will sink it. Is that clear enough?"

Sal placed his bullhorn on the wet ground by his feet, horn down, stood back up, straightened himself and then swung the 12.7 mm machine gun around so that it was pointed right at the cruise ship.

Tomas mentally counted down sixty seconds.

Ninety seconds later, the *Intrepid's* captain appeared on the swing deck about thirty feet above them. He too had a bullhorn in his hand. He held it up, causing it to squeak first. "We don't negotiate with terrorists. Leave now and our security will not shoot and destroy you." He put his bullhorn down and appeared to wait for Sal's reply.

Tomas knew this game. It was called the game of chicken. Whoever chickened out first and pulled their car aside before both cars careened into each other, head on, was the loser.

The captain's response must have incensed Sal, because he kicked the bullhorn, sending it clattering against the other side of the boat he couldn't see. Sal first aimed at the captain, but then lifted the barrel high in the sky, aiming the large gun over the ship. That way, the captain could see Sal was purposely trying to miss, but only this time: the equivalent of accelerating your car to force the other guy to chicken out faster. Sal fired, sending twenty tracer rounds over the *Intrepid's* bridge.

Tomas needed to end this game now, before it was too late.

He stepped out into the rain, slowly pacing to his boss, who had his back to him, all his attention focused on the *Intrepid's* swing deck.

Tomas focused on Sal's head, willing it to not turn back to him.

The rain hid his splashing footsteps, bathing the world around them in a loud, pattering drumbeat.

When Tomas was halfway from the bridge to Sal, he drew his Beretta, hidden beneath his shirt, and held it low and slightly behind him, so that Sal couldn't see it.

Sal huffed and murmured a fusillade of words under his breath, all of them not good. He was getting very angry again. This time, Sal swung the gun down, aiming the sight's crosshairs at the *Intrepid's* bow, right around its water line. The rounds were armor piercing, so Tomas imagined they'd go through their hull fairly easily. The *Intrepid* wouldn't survive if Sal fired the gun from bow to stern, even if he only sent over half of the rounds he was loaded for.

Tomas was three meters away now, raising his pistol and aiming directly at Sal's head.

Sal pulled back on the machine gun's charging bolt once again, readying the 12.7x108mm rounds for their intended destination, obviously figuring if he couldn't have this ship, he wouldn't let anyone else have it.

Two meters away, Tomas clicked the safety off.

"Really?" Sal yelled loud enough that Tomas could hear him in the rain. "Do you really think you could fool me, Tomas?"

Tomas halted, his arm starting to quiver, along with his nerve.

"I knew this was what you were planning..."—Tomas wasn't sure if he was pausing for effect or thinking out loud—"That's why I removed a round from the chamber... You'll now have to chamber a round before you can shoot and you know in that time, I can turn around and rip your throat out. Or Tomas, you can lay your gun down and join me."

Tomas thought about what Sal said, now unsure if Sal was bluffing or not. Tomas always checked the chamber of his weapon before he holstered it and Sal knew this. But Sal had him remove his weapon and holster earlier and Tomas was so nervous about hiding the gun under his shirt, he didn't remember checking it.

He pulled the trigger anyway.

The sound was hollow, but his bullet struck home with all the force he needed.

Sal's head buffeted back, but he didn't go down. Sal turned and faced him, his evil-looking eyes taunting him for more.

Tomas didn't hesitate. He put another round in Sal's head and four more into his body, until the man went down for good. Sal had been super-human, but he could still die like all humans.

Tomas dropped his Beretta, pulled his head up and immediately saw that a rifle was trained on him from the swing deck. He dropped down, ducking out of sight, and scooted over to the bullhorn.

He shook off its coating of water and held the bullhorn to his lips. "Please don't shoot me. I'm not one of them. He forced me to be here."

Raising up, unprotected by the hull, Tomas held both of his hands high in the air. He waited to be fired upon, not really caring anymore.

33

Four Orders

Jean Pierre made Tomas wait almost eight hours before allowing him to come aboard. It wasn't to punish or some sort of plan to wear down a potential combatant. Jean Pierre and his crew simply had a lot of work to do first, before they'd let anyone else on board.

In suite 8000, the captain convened his wardroom and invited his assistant security director and his environmental compliance officer to join them. He first discussed their preliminary status and then he went into his four orders, making sure they all understood and gave him their feedback. He sent them on their way and returned to the bridge.

At precisely, 10:30 AM, Jean Pierre stood in front of the ship's intercom and clicked the microphone button.

"Attention all crew of the Intrepid, both new and old. It is now safe to come out of your cabins as the danger has passed. I will address you all in the coming days and explain in more detail what has happened and what our situation is, but there is much work we must do right now.

"To this end, I have issued four orders to all of my crew, and that includes you. The first two have already been given to my most senior crew and they are executing them as I speak. The last two relate to everyone else who is currently on this ship.

"The four orders are as follows: first, to put a safe distance between us and the island's port; the second, to make sure we are properly fueled and then detached from the refueling barge on our starboard side; the third is to make sure there are no more combatants from the island or parasitics on board; and the fourth order is to clean up the mess.

"Because you are all a part of my crew and we are all in this together, I'm making you aware of all my orders. Again, only my third and fourth orders apply to everyone hearing this.

"We believe the immediate threat is over. The parasitics, which we had been holding in our Wayfarer Lounge, are no longer on the ship. Additionally, even though we let several on board, there should be no more guests from the island"—Jean-Pierre chose not yet to reveal their symptomatic nature—"on board.

"I won't lie to you; many have perished at the hands of the islanders and the parasitics. And many of them were killed as well. But the threat has passed.

"That's where you come in, and this leads to my third and fourth orders, which I am now giving to each of you.

"Everyone with a last name beginning with the letters A through L is on search patrol. Everyone with a last name beginning with the letters M through Z is on clean-up patrol.

"First, to the search patrol. Your job, beginning at the conclusion of this announcement, is to scour every cabin and every room on the entire ship, from deck 3 all the way up to the highest observation deck. You are looking for any islanders or parasitics. If you see either, alive or dead, do not engage them by yourselves. Call attention to any of our personnel wearing Regal European Blue. They will have our security staff toss them off the ship.

"For our clean-up patrol, your job is equally important. Besides cleaning up the debris in the areas that were damaged, so as to minimize any future hazards, you will also help us with identification and disposal of any bodies. If you find a dead body, please do not touch it yourselves. Report this to one of our personnel wearing Regal European Blue, and they will tell you what to do.

"Our personnel wearing Regal European Blue are already making their way to various locations. If you're unsure what to do, simply ask them.

"For both groups, consider this the ultimate scavenger hunt, where the prize is not a bottle of wine or fine dining, but all of our survival. Your work in the next few hours may be just that important.

"Those are my orders. As a member of my crew, I expect each of you to follow them. Thank you for your cooperation.

"This is your captain, Jean-Pierre Haddock. Out."

F lavio was tasked to lead a team to carry out the captain's first order: giving them a safe distance from Vila de Corvo's port. This order posed their biggest challenge. They certainly didn't want any more unauthorized boardings and having their port side moored to this dock left them too exposed and vulnerable. And that's where their challenge initially appeared greatest. On this, they realized quickly they had caught their biggest break.

Flavio had personally just dumped all of their parasitics out their exit and onto the dock, with another thirty parasitics, all of whom were hungry, angry and anxious to get back on board and make a meal out of his crew the moment they opened up their gangway again.

He was told that they couldn't just abandon the mooring lines, because they had a limited quantity of the specially designed rope on board and they had already cut one free when they had to flee the Port of Malaga.

And since there were no shoremen on the dock to disconnect the lines from the dock, that meant Flavio had to lead a capable team of men and women, only a few of whom were expert in detaching the heavy mooring ropes from dock's bollards, onto the dock.

Flavio wasn't sure what they would do if the parasitics swarmed the dock. And that's when he saw they had caught a giant-sized break. Before meeting his team at the port-side gangway on deck 2, Flavio first checked out the dock from the deck 10 outside running track.

The heavy downpour of cold rain must have driven away the mostly naked parasitics. They were now gone, except for a few bodies, and so was the rain.

Now, just before opening up the door, he checked once more with Ted on the radio, who had eyes on the dock from the port-side swing deck.

"Okay, open up, Ms. Johansson," Flavio stated, rifle at the ready.

The door slid open and Flavio stepped out onto the gangway bridge and searched their perimeter.

It was clean, other than the three dead parasitics and two dead islanders, who must have killed each other in the initial waylay. There were no other signs of anyone, anywhere.

He stepped up to the first body, giving it a kick, to make sure it wasn't faking it. In the distance, he heard something.

Flavio held a bald-fist up in the air, letting everyone know to be quiet and wait for him.

Mixed in with the growing commotion building on the ship, as their search and clean up teams started spreading out, finding their way topside, he heard something else. From the island, he heard an occasional scream or even grunt. He assumed this meant that their parasitics had gone on to feed on the rest of the islanders, who were probably easier to get to than the passengers of a sealed up, steel cruise ship.

He stepped over to the next body and gave it a kick. None of the others stirred, not even a little.

But then one did.

Flavio flipped off the rifle's safety and pointed at the clothed form on the deck, surrounded by a puddle of red. It was breathing. With his finger on the trigger, ready to put an end to its obvious suffering, he recognized quickly it was Ágúst Helguson, the parasitic who singlehandedly saved their ship.

Flavio cupped his hands around his mouth before he spoke, so that only those in the gangway could hear him. Just above a whisper, he said, "I need a medical team here."

He turned over the former second officer, who looked unconscious, but whose chest was still moving.

Three people, who represented their medical team, all recently recruited crew, took over and went to work on attempting to save the near dead man.

He's a parasitic, no longer a man, Flavio corrected himself in thought.

At the top of the gangway, he stated loud enough so all could hear, "Okay team, it is clear. Work quickly and quietly!"

W asano was charged with carrying out the captain's second order, making sure they were properly fueled and then detached from the refueling barge. It was also to protect their engineering chief, "at all costs."

The captain was concerned that they were running out of engineering personnel, since most had either been killed or had become monsters. As many as half of their remaining engineering staff died when toxic gas was released into the engine room by their own crew, in a traitorous attempt to kill the parasitics on board. When they were safe, Wasano planned to demand the captain hold a trial and punish any of those involved who were still alive.

The shortage in capable engineering crew meant that Niki Tesler, their punk-haired chief of engineering, was almost as important to their ship as the captain, when it came to crucial ship-knowledge which couldn't immediately be taught to someone else.

"Okay, first officer, can we get started?" Niki requested.

"Captain?" Wasano asked on his radio. His ear-piece immediately squawked back with the captain confirming from above that it was all clear.

"You're good to go, security chief."

The door opened with a gnawing creak, revealing a slaughter fest outside. There were over a dozen of their crew murdered and lying topside on the fueling barge. And as bitter a pill as it was, they were not going to collect these men and women and hold a proper burial at sea, like they did earlier for those who died during the first wave of attacks. Instead, one of their team was tasked with taking a picture of each dead crew member, for later identification, and then several of their team were tasked with tossing the bodies overboard.

The captain's orders were explicit when it came to this. There simply wasn't enough time. And their medical director said the bodies were too much of a health hazard to hold on board for later burial.

The rest of the team scurried out to each of the hoses, Niki behind them barking off directions to pull one hose off, which represented their heavy fuel. And then to attach the other hose, which was for their GMO. Niki told them that they had enough heavy fuel to last them for months, if they were judicious in its use. And so all they needed now was the GMO. They'd be done in less than an hour.

They had also decided to anchor the fueling barge off the dock and moor it to a mooring float, so that they'd have access to it later, if they needed it. There was no telling when they'd ever see another place to refuel.

As Wasano looked over the activity on the barge and most especially Niki, he didn't even want to consider the idea of returning to this place. As far as he was concerned, they couldn't leave soon enough.

34

After-Effects

Finally, when they had powered away from the Via de Corvo's dock and completed their search of the entire ship for the dead, confirming as well that there were no more parasitics or islanders on board, they invited the man they knew as Tomas Novo to board. He was promptly arrested.

Ted and TJ had been asked to be a part of their interrogation of Mr. Novo, so they could decide what to do with him after this. The security director and the captain would be conducting the interrogation.

Ted was the first to arrive at an unmarked room, next to the also unmarked brig, on deck 1, where they held the symptomatic islander whom Flavio and TJ had interrogated earlier.

While Ted waited for the others to arrive and for their "guest" to be escorted in, Ted reviewed his notes from the day. He planned to move these details into his log when he had a chance.

One thing bothered him, and he wanted to know the answer before anyone arrived. Each number in his notes, he mentally added to the last one, scratching a sub-total to the right of each number on the page. At the bottom of the second page, he wrote a final number and circled it. 215. That was preliminary number of reported dead their teams had found, which included both infected and non-infected, regardless of whether they died from the parasitic or islander attacks or succumbed to the toxic gas, or even somewhat more natural causes. These were rough numbers, but from what he remembered, that meant their total crew now, both existing and newly recruited, was somewhere south of four hundred.

He wondered how many crew it took to run a cruise ship this size, questioning if they had enough, even after the newly recruited were made useful.

The door clicked open and the captain walked in.

"Hello, captain," Ted welcomed.

"Ted," he acknowledged. His tone and face were of someone very tired and heavily burdened. It was the same look Jörgen had before he was viciously killed. Ted knew this to be true of any leader of a large group which experienced much hardship. And they certainly had.

The captain took a seat and glowered at Ted, like he wanted to tell him something horrible, but he wasn't sure if he was willing to at this point. But then, in a blink, he finally decided not to.

"How is your ankle?" the captain asked. His face and body language all at once were more relaxed, though he still showed concern.

"It's fine. I'm more concerned about TJ, and of course, all the others with much greater injuries than mine."

His face immediately switched back again to that of the leader who felt crushed by the burden of knowing some secret which caused him great pain. It hit Ted that whatever Jean Pierre was unwilling yet to tell him probably concerned his wife. And it was bad.

Jean Pierre tried to hide his emotions again, only partially masking his true mental state with a forced grin. "She's one of the toughest people I've ever met. She'll be fine. Doc Chloe says she's already healing, thanks to... well, whatever is happening to those infected like her."

"I know, I checked in on her earlier. Doc gave her a heavy sedative to knock her out for a while. That's why I'm surprised she was joining us on this... interview of our guest."

"We'll only need her for one purpose, to confirm whether or not Mr. Novo is a bad pear—"

"You mean apple."

"What?"

"You meant, whether or not Mr. Novo is a bad apple."

"Yes," his brow furrowed, and once again the whole complexion of the man changed. "And we can dispense with the pleasantries. This will be at minimum an interrogation and at worst an execution. You're here for one purpose too: yours is to observe and to render your opinion, only after we're done and only when I ask for it. I trust your opinion, Ted. But I will be the one who decides what happens to Mr. Novo. Are we clear?"

"Very."

The door opened, and in walked TJ, cleaned up and now wearing a light jacket, zipped up over her running outfit. Last time Ted saw her, she lay on a cot in their medical clinic, half asleep and still covered in dried blood, which was caked over her multiple scratches and two bandages covering her bullet wounds: one on her cheek and the other on her leg.

She limped in, assisted by crutches, looking dazed. "Hi Ted," she smiled and sat in the chair next to his. The only blood on her was that blood that still stained her nose plug, firmly clipped to her nose.

Before the door could close itself, Tomas Novo, in handcuffs, was led in by Wasano.

Mr. Novo was seated in a heavy chair in the center of the room. Wasano pulled out another set of handcuffs and clicked them around the chain of the handcuffs he already wore. The other end quickly clasped to the arm of the chair.

"I told you this is not necessary. I'm the one who killed Salvatore," pleaded Mr. Novo. His accent seemed strange. Ted guessed that was his Portuguese, with which Ted had little familiarity. "I will tell you whatever you want. Just please don't send me back to that island. I've been trying to leave it ever since I was sent there."

Their interrogation, which turned out to be more of an interview, went well as the man gave them every detail about how he first came to the island as a lowly deputy, or what they called an agent. And how he'd been trying to get transferred to Lisbon, but his boss wouldn't let him leave the island.

Then he told them about the barge that crashed into their town and how over three-quarters of their town went crazy or at least showed signs of the Rage disease.

Tomas said that he wasn't completely opposed to Salvatore's methods to segregate the infected from those who were not infected, like him.

Each time Mr. Novo mentioned the infected or what he called crazy-people or the Rage disease, he'd eyeball TJ, who remained quiet the entire time, only twice pulling off her nose clip, sniffing and then turning to the captain with a head shake, which Ted guessed meant that Mr. Novo wasn't infected.

Tomas said that he noticed that his boss's behavior had been changing, that he showed less compassion and constant anger. One night, Mr. Novo said he followed his boss and witnessed him torture and murder a man who was showing signs of the disease. It was also the first time he saw that his boss was one of them, with red eyes and pale skin, just not as out of control as the others.

Before this, he had just assumed his boss was fighting a cold.

Mr. Novo then went on to the elaborate plan that his boss and two other men had come up with to lure in a ship, like the *Intrepid*, pretending that they were offering fuel for food, when in fact, the offer of fuel was only to trap a ship and hold the people for food.

He'd been trying to find a way to leave them, but he was under the constant threat of death. It wasn't until he was alone with his boss that he found a way to stop him.

Wasano showed him a picture of the squat islander TJ had tortured earlier and then interrogated with Flavio. Then, he had heard from Flavio that the islander boasted about the plot that Mr. Novo just confirmed. Mr. Novo not only ID'd the men, he gave them the names and details of these men.

"So where did you get the military ship?" asked the captain.

"Oh, you mean the P114?" asked Mr. Novo. "My boss stole it from the closed military base on the other side of the island."

"The former US military base, closed years back?" the captain asked.

"Yes. We were looking at the base as a place where we could keep the crazy people separated from the ten or so regular townspeople, like me, and the fifteen or so men, like Salvatore, who showed signs of the Rage.

"We went there a few days ago and happened to arrive the same time as that patrol boat. We're not sure where it came from, because Salvatore and his men killed the two military guys and took the boat. He told me it was to limit the threat and because he really wanted the boat." Tomas was looking down at his handcuffs and then had a thought. "Hey, you can have the boat if you want. I can show you how to work it." He glanced at the captain. "Although you probably already know how."

"Did you find any supplies there?" Ted asked, forgetting he was supposed to be quiet and just listen.

"Not that I saw, or was told, but the whole base was intact. And it didn't look like the tsunami damaged it at all. I wondered why we never used it for the crazy people. Until your ship answered Salvatore's call. Then, only after he released them today, did I understand why he wanted them kept close."

Mr. Novo fell silent, but so did everyone else.

Because it was the captain's show, everyone looked to him, waiting for some cue as to what he wanted to ask next.

Jean Pierre's eyes were drilled into the floor in front of him, his face drawn down into a scowl, like he was calculating something in his head. Then he arrived at an answer, his head popped back up and he asked, "Mr. Novo, will you take us to this base tomorrow?"

35

News

TJ Williams frowned at her reflection in the mirror. She was already getting used to the stranger staring back at her each morning, but she wasn't used to all of the added effort she had to go through to cover it up for the benefit of others. Dabbing at her lips with Hollywood Red, her preferred shade of gloss—*actually their preferred shade*—she tried to figure out some sensation which seemed out of place. It began in her stomach. This quickly grew into a scratchy feeling in her throat. She swallowed back the raw bitterness, like something trying to come up. "Oh no." She bent over and puked in her sink.

"What the hell?" she asked herself, pushing up from the cool basin, holding back the next wave of nausea that wanted to take possession of her. She scrutinized herself once again in the mirror, focused on every detail or nuance in her face, looking for some sign to tell her what was going on. *Am I getting sick?* she wondered.

As she examined her tongue for spots, her neck for swelling, her head for heat, she began to panic. Illness for people who were symptomatic meant a fever. A fever meant becoming parasitic. She did not want to turn into one of those things, not after fighting so hard to remain human.

She thought she had become one, when she took those men's lives, consumed some of their blood and then almost attacked her husband. But Wasano's bullet brought her back. She wanted to avoid another episode, at all costs.

A quick look at her clock confirmed she could make it to the medical clinic before she met with JP, who had something important to tell her before they sent a team in to inspect the military base. She would thankfully sit that one out and maybe take some time to apologize to her husband. The last three times he'd seen her, she was either crazy or drugged.

Doing a final check of her look and outfit, she noticed right away she'd forgotten her contacts. *No time,* she told herself. She'd wear sunglasses; otherwise she looked fine.

The sunglasses went over her eyes and she slipped out the door, now only needing one crutch to move around. She bounded down the hallway, so focused she didn't even hear Jaga yelling her name from a cabin door close to hers.

In the two minutes it took her to drop down the two decks and get into the RE Medical Center door, the nausea had a firm grip over her once again.

"**W**hat is it?" Vicki asked. She flopped her head up to look at him, her eyes expectant, a giant smile was plastered her face. Flavio thought then, if she didn't like the gift, it was worth it just for that look.

"Maybe you open up and you find out," Flavio stated, trying to make his words sound matter-of-fact, as if this box wasn't anything more important than a lost hairbrush he'd found or a stick of her favorite bubblegum. But it was something he knew she would love.

"I can't believe you bought me a prezzie." Vicki flashed him another smile and turned to address the box. Each of box's flap corners were tucked in under the next, loosely sealing the top closed, but for a small square hole in the middle. She stuck her forefinger into the hole and felt something soft. And then that something moved.

She pulled her finger out and glowed at him. "You didn't?"

Flavio shrugged. At this point, he just wished she'd just open the damned box.

The box meowed at her.

She opened it up, reached in and pulled out Cat, immediately plowing her face into its soft belly, Cat purring in response.

"Watch out. She has sharp claws and—are you all right?"

She held the cat under her chin, like she was using it as a chin-rest. She stared at Flavio, tears flowing from her eyes. "How did you know I missed my kitty so much? I think I mentioned her only once to you."

He just smiled, remembering when she had told him how much she missed her cat. Why spoil it with words, his mother used to tell him.

"Flavio Petrovich, I think I may be in love with you." She leaned over to him and kissed him softly.

"Where did you find her?" She sniffled.

"It followed me inside, after climbing up my leg."

She sniffled some more. "Look at me, blubbering like a baby."

She put Cat back into its box and looked up at him, her face serious. "Okay, so tell me you'll be safe?"

"I will."

She hugged him, unwilling to let go.

"I promise," he said, meaning it.

"And thank you, Flavio."

He felt like fist-pumping right now, but he knew that would be a little much. So he offered a simple "You're welcome," kissed her again, and walked out the door. Then once it closed, he dashed down the hallway and up the stairwell. He was going to be late for a private meeting with the captain, if he didn't hurry. He smiled the whole way.

He made it to cabin 8000 with a minute to spare and reached to knock on the door, just as Mrs. TJ Williams was coming out. She glanced up at him, surprised he was there, tears streaking her face. She hesitated in between him and the doorway, as if she was shell-shocked. She looked completely unsure of what she was supposed to do next.

"Mrs. Villiams, are you okay?"

She remained that way, not responding. And Flavio had no idea what he could do to help or comfort her. Unlike Vicki crying tears of joy, this woman was very upset about something she heard or saw.

"I..." Her gaze fell back down, like the words were stuck behind her tongue and she couldn't figure out how to unstick them. She looked up again. "I'm sorry." She then turned and walked off, dragging her crutch behind her.

He watched her move away, shocked himself at what he saw. This woman was one of the strongest he'd ever met, but at that moment, she looked helpless.

Flavio now considered the fact that he was meeting the captain next and he was likely to hear whatever the captain had told Mrs. Williams, and the reason for her distress.

Flavio was rarely nervous about anything. But at this moment, he felt his stomach turn loops.

He knocked. "Captain? It's Flavio Petrovich."

"Please come in, Flavio."

He did.

"Flavio, please sit down. I need to tell you something that only three other people currently know, but it will affect everyone on this ship."

36

The Island

L ess than an hour later, TJ, Flavio and Wasano left on the P114 military craft, piloted by Mr. Novo, to the other side of the island to inspect Layes military base. Ted didn't know this at first, only that TJ never showed up for their breakfast date at 8AM. He asked around and no one knew where she was. When he went to her cabin, she didn't answer. The only person who had seen her was Jaga, their room attendant when they first boarded, and now in a cabin next to TJ's temporary cabin on deck 3. Jaga said only that she seemed upset and was limping away as fast as she could and didn't hear him calling her. Jaga also said he was sure that TJ had gone "downstairs."

There were only two destinations she'd have any business with downstairs: deck 2's exits or deck 1 and the RE Medical clinic. He had heard the military boat leave, but she didn't indicate anything about being on it, so he concluded she must have gone to the clinic. And Jaga said that she looked upset and in a hurry. Maybe she was sick. That's when he became worried.

Now Ted was dashing down the stairs and through the small deck 1 public area to see Chloe in Medical.

Ted heard her voice when he knocked.

"Oh Ted, I'm glad you're here. I wanted to talk to you about my results for the T-Gondii blood test. Do you have a few minutes?"

Ted watched her carefully, not answering right away. He had been working with her regarding the parasitics, running ideas and theories back and forth. She was incredibly bright and would have made a brilliant doctor, if their normal world hadn't ended. Instead, this young woman was receiving one of the finest crash-course educations on medicine.

She looked up from her notes to see why he hadn't answered.

"Did you see my wife today?" he asked, scrutinizing how she responded next.

She looked down and away from him—a sure sign she was hiding something. "Ah, yes, I did. But..." She hesitated and gave him a tentative glance, "you really should talk to her."

"What's wrong? Is she all right?" He was really getting worried.

"She's fine, just a little nausea."

"Nausea?" He looked up, trying to remember if other symptomatics complained of nausea, other than at the onset of a fever, and that was not good. "Are you sure she's okay?"

"I'm sure."

"Okay, can you at least tell me where she is now?"

"I only know that she went to see the captain after me. She had an appointment with him, in fact."

"Thank you." Ted turned to leave.

"Ted, what about my data on the Toxo test?"

He would normally have been interested, but he had only one thing on his mind: his wife. Ted gave her a smile. "Sorry. Maybe later?"

The P114 drafted with ease through the waves tossed up from the windward side of the island.

Tomas drove them around a breaker wall into a small bay with a beach, but no dock. Lush trees surrounded both sides of the beach and the rest of the area was thick with vegetation growing all around multiple buildings that spread out over a large area. A giant fence appeared to bisect part of the island, separating this base from the larger section of land stretched all the way around to the other side, where they left the *Intrepid* anchored. Apparently, no road on the mostly rural island connected the two sides.

Flavio looked back at Mrs. Williams, who seemed to be gazing out into nowhere.

He thought about what the captain said and thought about her and all of the others who would be affected. He couldn't imagine what she was thinking right now. He felt such sorrow for her and Mr. Williams.

They beached only a couple of minutes later.

Flavio gazed at Mrs. Williams and her leg, where he understood Wasano had shot her to keep her from attacking them. She still favored it, although less than he would have expected. But now Flavio had such empathy for her, he worried about her getting it wet.

"Mrs. Villiams, can I help you to the—"

She didn't wait for him to finish, jumping off the boat into the water, which was chest-level on her. She thrust a full canvas bag above her head.

Flavio jumped in next, holding his rifle above his head before plunging in, soaking himself up to his waist. He turned back to see his security director doing the same thing as him, only he was almost completely submerged.

For a moment Flavio wondered if Mr. Novo was going to leave them there, stranded. But he too jumped out, carrying a rope attached to the bow. He lumbered through the water, then up to the beach and tied the line to a piling attached to a large rock, just out of the water. He'd obviously been here before, just as he had said.

Once they were all of the water, Mrs. Williams called to them, "Come on, let's get started."

The captain's instructions were to follow her around and make sure the place was clear of parasitics or other threats and that it was securable.

She retrieved a clipboard and pen from the top of her soft canvas bag. Immediately she started scribbling notes on the pre-printed pages.

As they went from building to building, she furiously dashed down notes, occasionally asking one of them to assist her with a measurement.

Wasano left Flavio and Mrs. Williams alone while he walked the entire fence line to make sure there were no breaches.

For the next two hours, Flavio continued to keep an eye on their surroundings, sometimes vaulting himself into crawl spaces or inspecting dark corners and generally assisting her with whatever she asked. She seemed to know exactly what she was looking for.

When she was done, they sat on the stoop of one of the houses nearest the beach and waited for the security director to return. Meanwhile, she examined her notes and he watched her. He couldn't help but say something.

"I feel such sadness for you, Mrs. Villiams."

She looked up at him, laying her clipboard aside. She was no longer wearing her sunglasses, either losing them or finding no more need in wearing them to hide her eyes. Besides, it was a dark and overcast day. Her reddish eyes no longer looked eerie or horrific. To Flavio, they looked beautiful but burdened.

"Please Flavio," she said softly. "After all we've been through together, would you do me the favor of calling me by my first name or just TJ?"

He nodded.

Ever so tenderly, she laid her hand on his. "I know you know why we're here. And soon everyone else will know. I also suspect, by your comment, that you must know about my personal situation. I'm asking you to please say nothing to my husband. I want to tell him myself."

He tried to grin, but his frown didn't want to budge. "Captain made me swear not to mention it, even to Vicki. I'll keep your secret, Mrs... Teresa Jean."

"It's better this way, you know... for everyone."

She smiled at him, but he knew it was covering up her own sadness.

He wanted to comfort her. And if they had been like this any longer, he would have. But right then, he heard Wasano trudging back along the beach.

She released her hands from his.

Wasano signaled for them to meet him in the boat and Flavio waved back, acknowledging this.

She watched him as he stood up and he then offered to help her up, but she shook her head.

And then he knew.

"You aren't coming back with us, are you?"

"No, I'm not, Flavio. There's lots of preparation needed. And I want to get a head start on it."

Flavio looked back at the boat and then at her. "Will you be all right?"

"Yes, I will." She held out her hand and Flavio held out his, thinking she was going to shake his, but she pulled herself up so that she was standing toe to toe with him. She leaned up and kissed him on his cheek.

"You're a good man, Flavio. The ship is lucky to have you. Look after my husband, will you?"

He gave her a weak grin and nodded.

She sat back down on the stoop and waved at him.

He turned back to the boat, slowly making his way through the sand and then the water.

Taking a hand from Mr. Agarwal, he hoisted himself up onto the boat. At the same time Mr. Novo, who had already brought in the mooring line, started up the engine and reversed them back into the bay.

As they turned in the bay to head back to their ship, Flavio watched TJ Williams—*Teresa Jean,* he corrected himself.

She was still sitting on that stoop, staring out at the beach.

It was the last time he saw her.

37

The Meetings

After Flavio said goodbye to Teresa Jean, he considered what had happened to the world, in light of what that meant for Teresa Jean and Ted. He then vowed to himself to never let anything go unsaid between Vicki and him. And when he returned to the ship, he literally ran to Vicki's cabin, proclaimed his love to her and asked her to marry him. Even though he wanted to tell her what had happened, he could not reveal the truth until after the captain's message was delivered four days later. On that morning, everyone would know the basic truth, including Ted.

Each day since Flavio's return, two tenders of men—all of whom only knew a little of the truth, but were all sworn to secrecy—along with food, bulk materials and other supplies were transported to the island. Each day, the tenders would return with just the men.

Each man, upon return to the ship, was escorted back to their cabins on deck 2, where they ate and slept, isolated from the rest of the ship, and under the watch of armed guards. The only other crew member allowed into that section of the ship was Buzz at the same time the first tenders were sent out, only so that the monitor cameras could be disconnected. Their mission was kept hidden from everyone.

Meanwhile, the *Intrepid* was slowly being cleaned and fixed up as teams of crew members worked tirelessly to bring her back to full functionality. Everyone was working on something, night and day, so that there was little time for anything but eating and sleeping.

Flavio was tasked during the day with training new recruits to become security. During the afternoons and evenings, he held personal defense classes for the whole ship. Often forty or fifty attended each of the two classes.

He was given the freedom to teach as he wanted, but the captain had told him to focus on giving each crew member the tools to take care of themselves if a parasitic attacked. He did as instructed, using his personal knowledge of going toe-to-toe with some of those things. But he knew it probably wouldn't do any good: as fast as they were now, Flavio was pretty sure in most every circumstance, it was a losing proposition against one. And there'd be no chance against two or more. The only tool that worked and gave you a fighting chance was an automatic weapon, like his. But since there were only three automatic weapons on the whole ship, Flavio had to do his best instructing them how to use knives and clubs.

Still, all who attended thanked him, saying they just wanted to feel safe and in control, and he gave them that power with his instruction. Flavio had to admit that this filled him with immeasurable pride.

Every moment Flavio wasn't working or sleeping, he spent with Vicki, treating each like it might be their last. That was the secret gift that Teresa Jean gave him and he hoped Vicki would be the benefactor of TJ's gift as well.

The whole time, he thought about Ted and Teresa Jean during the quiet moments or just before sleep, when Flavio was forced to deal with his own guilt.

Two days before the meetings was the only time he had seen Ted. They were passing along the promenade deck, going in opposite directions. Flavio watched Ted, but Ted stared into space, marching at his usual quick pace—his limp from his sprained ankle was almost imperceptible now. Flavio had to step in front of him, because Ted was so lost in his thoughts that he didn't even hear his own name. Flavio wanted to let Ted be, but he needed to talk to him, even though he didn't know what to say, because he really couldn't say anything.

"How are you, Mr. Villiams?"

He gave Flavio a vacant stare. "You know... And would you please call me Ted? After all we've been through together."

Flavio smiled at the memory of being asked the same thing by Teresa Jean. "Your wife... She..." He couldn't bear to say it. He couldn't say it without revealing more than he should. "Please let me know if you need something, Ted."

Ted nodded, gave him a little smile and walked away.

Like any known moment in the future, neither work nor joyous play could slow down the steady march of time. The day he dreaded was now. The morning of the meetings arrived.

Flavio was to be at the meeting run by the captain. Ted was to run the other.

The announcement came at 7:30AM, just as previous announcements and fliers had warned all crew to be prepared to listen then. The captain stated that there would be two mandatory meetings held in thirty minutes. The one held in the Wayfarer Lounge, which had been miraculously cleaned out and ready in time, was to be attended by everyone whose cabins were in the aft half of the ship, from the mid-way stairwell to the stern. The second meeting, held simultaneously, was in the Tell Tale

Theatre, and was to be attended by all cabin holders from the forward stairwell to the bow.

No one but Flavio, Wasano, Ted, the captain and now all but five of their security personnel, which had blossomed to twenty-five, knew the content of the meetings' message. Rumors had spread that it had something to do with the military base, especially since many could see the tenders going back and forth. And certainly those crew who saw the supplies being loaded could surmise that the men who were traveling on the tenders and kept in isolation were making the military base habitable. But for what, they didn't know. Flavio was amazed that the captain kept this secret so under wraps.

As the people filed into each room, his security personnel's job was to get them to their seats quickly and quietly. Thirty minutes prior, immediately after the announcement, some of his security personnel had gone to each of the aft cabins to make sure their occupants attended the meeting in the lounge.

Other security corralled the few stragglers into their respective rooms, so that on the hour, it appeared to Flavio, that everyone was where they should be.

At that moment, Flavio for the captain's meeting and Wasano for Ted's meeting, locked the main entrance doors, so that no one could leave until it was time.

Ted marched over to the lectern on the stage, taking quick measure of his audience. All looked nervous. He wasn't. It seemed like another lifetime ago when he was often filled with overwhelming panic at having to speak to a large group. Now this felt like an old hat: snug, comfortable, ready to do its job. The speaking wasn't the issue; it was the dread of delivering this message. He'd been dreading this since the day the captain told him what was going to happen next. At that moment, he put on his speaker's hat and delivered.

"Good morning." He paused to make sure everyone was paying attention. They needed to hear what came next.

"My name is Ted Williams and I'm here on behalf of our captain, Jean Pierre Haddock, to make a special announcement that affects everyone on this ship. At the same time I am speaking to you, the captain is delivering almost the same announcement on the other side of the ship.

"First, so you know, the ship has all of the fuel it needs and we've removed the island threat." Normally Ted would have paused here to allow this good piece of news to sink in. But he moved directly into the first part of the secret he'd been carrying.

"Additionally, the threat of parasitics attacking on board is behind us... for now. It's true, we have removed the parasitics from our ship, but the parasitic threat still dwells here. That's because anyone who is infected with the Toxo parasite can become parasitic the moment their body temperature rises to ninety-nine degrees. Many of us have witnessed this firsthand, with a passenger seemingly okay one minute and then the next minute, they seem crazy, with murder on their minds.

"Today we will remove that threat from this ship for good. All of you in this room are currently staying in forward cabins, but your being invited to this specific place wasn't for your convenience. It was for one simple reason: none of you are currently infected with the parasite."

J ean Pierre paused to let it sink in.

"Yes, what I'm telling you is true. Everyone in this room is currently infected with the Toxo parasite. Many of you know this and have known this. But for some of you, this is the first time you've heard this, because you may not be symptomatic yet. Then again, a few of you are already symptomatic and you've noticed the tell-tale signs like the red eyes, pale skin, thoughts of violence, confusion and unreasonable anger."

The room filled with murmurs and mumblings from almost everyone in the room.

Jean Pierre stopped and held up his hands. And when they didn't immediately settle down he yelled, "Quiet! Listen. Every single one of you will, at some point in the future, experience some or all of these symptoms. And as someone who is infected, when your body temperature hits ninety-nine degrees, you may become parasitic. And if you do, you would be a threat to everyone on this ship who is not infected. And that means you are a threat to this ship.

"As the captain of the Intrepid, I cannot allow this threat to persist on my ship. Therefore, I have arranged for temporary shelters and supplies for each of you at a secure military base on the other side of this island. We will begin moving you there in a few minutes. Your personal belongings have already been packed up for you and are waiting on a tender, which will deliver you and your belongings to the island. And before you ask, this is not negotiable." He took a deep breath. "If you do not comply or you resist leaving this ship, you will be shot. Please begin leaving now. You will be escorted by our security now.

At that moment, Flavio clicked open the door lock and hollered, "Follow this man right here, now."

A security guard held up a sign that had a number 1 on it. Other guards had placards with other numbers on their signs.

T ed held up his hands to quiet the crowd.
"People... This is happening right now."
The theater was filled with whispers, weeping and a few angry comments. Two people rose from their seats and started to march toward the entrance, but Wasano took a step in front of them and pointed his rifle. The intent was clear: you intend to interfere, you will be shot.

"Everyone, remain seated until this announcement is over. Security is now walking down the aisles, passing out lists of those people infected who are moving to the island. If you don't find a name on the list, then that person is not infected. If a family member or a loved one is one of those who is infected and therefore going to the island and you are not infected, you will not be allowed to accompany them to the island. This is for your safety and the safety of those on the island. At some point in the future, we will set up a method of visitation to the island. Believe me when I say this was a hard decision which affects everyone."

Ted was about to say, "My wife is there too." But he didn't want to blur the line. It was true, he'd suffered by being separated from her since she'd nearly died and become symptomatic. And he hadn't seen her since she was on the island preparing it and planning to help those who were infected and forced to go there, so they could prepare for their life as an infected person.

But then Ted expected her to return to the ship, as the one exception to the captain's rule, not only because she had proven herself multiple times, but because they still needed someone symptomatic to be able to periodically sniff-test each of their crew to make sure no one became infected, no matter how unlikely that might be.

38

New Life (51 Days Later)

Flavio came home to find his wife Vicki standing just inside the door, wearing a giant smile and the short blue dress he loved.

"Ahh... Hello," Flavio responded, his smile only crawling up one cheek. "Did I do something?"

She snickered, "Well yeah, I'd say you did."

She held out her hands and he accepted them.

"Come here." She led him into their cabin, body-blocking something she didn't yet want him to see. When she moved to the side, she revealed their coffee table covered in a checkered tablecloth, with near formal settings, including nice silverware, two covered plates—he could see they were heated—and a Guinness beer, with beads of sweat rolling down its neck. He could smell the delightful Thai spices in the air.

"Did you do something?" he asked sure that something was wrong; otherwise she wouldn't have gone to such trouble.

"Yes, I did!" she proclaimed, practically hopping. "What's that at the edge of the table?" she asked playfully.

He looked at her and then at the table and now saw something there. He walked over and picked up the only foreign-looking object from her table setting.

Then it hit him. He snapped his head back to Vicki and now her entire face was enveloped with a smile. "Does this mean..."

She nodded, hopped twice and then leapt onto him. "We're preggers."

He spun her around, but then thought twice about it, letting her down easily. "Sorry. You must be careful now."

She punched him in the arm. "You can be so daft sometimes. I'm fine. Ohh, and that's not the only big news."

Flavio was already feeling lightheaded about her pregnancy announcement. He wasn't sure he could take any other big news.

"Come here." She grabbed his paw and led him to the bathroom.

"What?"

"Take a peek, but don't be too loud; you don't want to wake them."

He screwed his mug at her, like she was playing some sort of gotcha game and he was about to walk into it.

"Go on..." she insisted.

If it makes her happy, especially in her condition, he thought and pulled open the bathroom door.

In the corner, where they had been keeping Cat—she insisted on calling it Liz—was not only Cat, but five little kittens.

"Isn't that cute? Liz had little babies."

All Flavio could think of was how they were going to hide six cats now; one was hard enough.

"Can you put in a request for a family cabin now, or do we have to wait until little Flavio is born?"

He ignored her request. Of course he'd put in the request. But something struck him as odd.

He stepped into the bathroom and knelt down to closely examine Momma Cat and her kittens that were blindly suckling on her. Cat looked over to Flavio and meowed at him and he saw it again. It was one of her eyes: it had turned red.

T he tender slashed at the surging sea and Ted tried not to feel nauseous, not usually getting seasick, especially after living on a ship for over two months. But he knew it was not just the rocking seas that jolted his sense of balance; it was the thought of seeing his wife after two months. But that wasn't all.

It was the sense that this meeting, rather than being a joyous celebration, was instead a goodbye.

Ted was no idiot. He knew that they had no need for a symptomatic on their ship anymore: Chloe had fully developed a blood test for the Toxo infection. A simple prick of a finger and a little droplet of blood was all that was needed and already the captain had ordered mandatory testing once every two months for everyone on board. And those who tested positive would be escorted to the island.

So the only reason why TJ could return to them was eliminated by Chloe's new test. But Ted still held out hope.

The captain had even agreed that she could come on board and stay for short visits. It wasn't a permanent solution, but it was a start. But only if he could convince her to come back.

Their last conversation on the radio told him she was thinking otherwise. She was cold and seemed unconvinced by his logic.

The boat came down hard off the crest of a large wave, rattling his bones in the process.

Ted looked up and saw the ring of the beach, past the breaker wall, almost completely covered in dots: no doubt the residents waiting to greet all of the visitors on their first visitation tender since the infecteds were relocated fifty-one days ago.

He glanced back and saw all the happy faces pointing at the beach, some even waving, as if they could see their spouses, loved ones or friends from this distance.

Ted returned his gaze, trying to do the same thing and sort out which one was his wife.

TJ always stood out in the crowd to him, even if she wasn't the most glamorous or the most classically beautiful. Most would consider her a beautiful woman and many had made comments to him and to her about her features over the years. But to Ted, her beauty and presence was so much more than that. She had a radiance that shone brighter than any physical beauty could.

Pretty quickly, he could identify her, standing alone at the top of the beach's littoral plain. She was covered in a hooded white robe that whipped around in the wind.

Ted found that his heart was racing, beating so hard it hurt for him to take breaths. He couldn't wait to hold her, to gaze into her strange new eyes and see the love she'd always held for him.

The tender slid onto the beach and a crewman tossed a line to a waiting person, who tied it off on a pylon to the left of TJ. She stood there stoically, a pylon more unmovable looking than the inanimate post beside her.

Ted was the first off, hopping with both feet into the water, not caring about getting wet. He shuffled through the water, then ran up the beach, desiring to the embrace her. He dashed by others, as if they didn't exist; his gazed was glued to her.

Still she remained, unmoving and seemingly unaffected by him.

When he was a countable number of steps away, a glint of light illuminated the darkness inside her hoodie that otherwise shrouded her head from him. He caught just a glimpse of her familiar smile creep up her unfamiliar face.

He halted only a few feet from her, because she still hadn't moved. *Was she unwilling or unable?* His squinted to see more inside the covered murk of her hooded robe, for another glimmer of his wife, standing there in this foreign form.

Finally, she lifted her hands up to the hood's edges and pulled it back to reveal her newly striking features. It was purposeful and it sucked his breath away.

Her hair was cut short, just over her ears and it was ghostly white-colored, like fine strands of silk; her eyelashes, thinned to the point of being hidden against her skin were also white; her skin's pigment was completely bleached away; her lips, also almost invisible; both her eyes blazed like two blood moons cast against pools of white. And yet, they were the two most beautiful eyes he had ever seen.

A teardrop fell out of one of them. Then another. And another, until they both showered like a summer rainstorm.

"Oh, Ted," she cried and in a single bound, she leapt onto him, wrapping her arms around him.

Not expecting this, he almost fell backwards, but he dug in and held tight to her slight frame, not wanting to let go. Her lips found his and they remained passionately locked for one all-consuming breath.

And then she released herself, exhaled and pushed away from him. He let go and she dropped into the sand and stepped back, breathing heavily while wiping at her eyes.

Normally tears would have streaked her makeup, but she wasn't wearing any. Her face almost instantly returned to its natural state just before the tears, without any normal rosy flare in her cheeks or any of the other tell-tale signs that she had cried. It was like it didn't happen, even though he could still taste the proof of their saltiness from that moment.

Her robe had opened some during their embrace and the wind whipped up again attempting to open it further. She immediately subdued it before more of her was exposed, palming her belly softly with one hand and tugging roughly with the other at it, where it criss-crossed her bust. Underneath the robe she was wearing a sleeveless olive T, rather than her usual—at least it was usual when he last saw her—sports bra. Most noticeably missing against her pale chest was her Orion necklace that he had given her over two months ago for their anniversary.

His eyes must have been hanging there too long, because she pulled with both hands now on the robe's edges, covering herself to her neck. "I lost it," she blurted. "The new chain you gave me broke." She said this without emotion, as if she were speaking about something that was meaningless.

He really didn't care about the necklace, not much anyway. But he couldn't help but feel like it meant something, a metaphor for their relationship... *Was it truly broken? Lost?*

Almost in reply, barely loud enough to be heard over the excited chaos around them from loved ones and friends embracing, just like they had been too many moments ago, she said, "I'm not going back with you. I have to stay here."

There it was, now stated in no uncertain terms. And as much as her words hit him like a punch to his solar plexus, he knew this was how it had to be.

Even if she agreed to come back with him, she'd never be allowed to stay. And it was foolish for even him to think this. She might still be his wife and it was obvious that she loved him, as evidenced by her tears and passionate embrace, but that didn't change what she was now: a predator, who could no more occupy his cabin than a leopard.

Her delicate lips opened slightly, quivered, but then held firm. Then they quivered again before she said, "You know I'm still in love with you?"

He smiled. "Yeah, I'm sure of that." He wanted to ask her something, but he wasn't sure how to. "Are you... Okay? I mean, are you happy here?"

Now she smiled. And it was genuine.

"Yes, I'm fine. And for the first time since this whole thing started, I'm at peace."

Ted couldn't help but cast a questioning glance, because he really didn't understand. But he desperately wanted to. He was trying to think how to ask it, when she volunteered to help him understand.

"I had thought it was some sort of inner evil—that I was evil and that part of me was trying to take over my humanity. It's not. I'm not evil and it's not an evil being: it's just a disease that was making changes in me. And yes, these changes brought temptations of doing evil things. And at times, they were overwhelming and felt uncontrollable. But I always had a choice, just like I did before I was infected. I chose not to do evil things to others. I chose not to be a monster. Anyone afflicted with this can also make that choice.

"And Ted, I'm helping others here to make the right choice. Some have chosen the easiest way, and they often end up becoming monsters; others have chosen the harder path. It's always their choice.

"The disease does change you in many ways, both physically and physiologically, as we both know. In a way, it's just like say, cataracts changing your eyesight. Barring some sort of surgery, you'd have to just adjust to your new condition. In our case though, the condition offers some benefits too and we have to adjust to them all." She hesitated, her eyes getting watery again.

"None of this changes my feelings for you. My heart will always belong to you and to you alone... But I also know we can't be together, like we were."

"I understand," he said. "It's not just us. There's no possible union for infected and non-infected people... But it still hurts."

"For me too... We can still visit, like this. I do want to see you again."

"Okay."

They held onto their silence for a while. It was not unlike so many of their times together in the past, when they'd talk for hours and just stop and enjoy their silence together.

But this too couldn't last.

"I need to go. I'm working with Boris and Penny, who are having a difficult time coping with the changes she's going through."

"Until the next visit then," Ted said, stepping into her with his lips pursed.

She reflexively scrunched up her nose, obviously attempting not to smell him. But she kissed him softly and then quickly turned and ran the other way, into the village.

He watched her disappear behind a stand of trees, then into the arms of Penny, who was standing with her husband on the stoop of one of the many buildings clustered around the beach.

Ted breathed out a long sigh. This wasn't the life he wanted, but it was one he could accept. He would count the days until his next trip here.

Until then, he knew everything would be all right.

Epilogue

Four Years Later

Ted rubbed the gray beard carpeting his face, while keeping his other hand tightly on the tender's wheel. The waves were extra choppy today so he had to keep a tight hold of the rudder. They'd lost one of their tenders a year ago, killing their pilot and another crew member, not to mention dumping their supplies into the ocean. The captain said the rudder probably got away from him in the cross current. Ted wasn't about to be another one of the *Intrepid's* many casualties.

This month's load of supplies was similar to what he brought on most of his trips. Salt and some other recyclables. For the first two years, they were exporting their food supplies to the colony. But now it was the other way around. They would receive fresh meat from the livestock that the colony tended, fruit from their orchards and vegetables from their gardens.

Today, he had a new addition for their colony—the first person in memory who had developed an infection and then become symptomatic. The young boy, named Pasquale, sat alone in his thoughts, at the back of the tender, only Ted and a security guard—there for Ted's protection—to look after him. But soon Pasquale would be with his own people. They would teach him about living a life with this disease. If Pasquale was lucky, he'd get Ted's wife as a teacher. Ted prayed this would happen for the boy and TJ.

Once he maneuvered the boat around the breaker wall and into the bay, Ted did what he always did before each visit: he scanned the beach for his wife. There were quite a few colonists on the beach today, much more than normal. They must be there for Pasquale's benefit, to make him feel welcome.

Ted had gotten quite good at his landings, cutting the engine and drafting the boat to the same place each time. As he stepped carefully out and around to the bow, grabbing the coiled line, he saw several familiar faces waiting. Some waved at him.

Ted tossed his line and it was grabbed and tied off when the boat stopped. Ted hopped off from the bow, barely splashing at the waterline's edge.

Ágúst was the first person to greet him, his welcoming smile always genuine and wide. It was still hard to believe he survived the beating he took, though every time Ted saw him, his skin looked paler.

Frans was there as well, and so was Jaga. Little Taufan, who was all white now and apparently didn't run around much anymore, was at home nestled in his arms. Both wore big smiles as well. He noticed right away that Frans' eyes were like two bright cherries. Ted had heard that he'd become symptomatic and was following Ágúst and TJ's spiritual guidance. Jaga looked no different than before and he was glad for that. He'd never become symptomatic.

Ágúst motioned to Ted for the mail bag, which he almost forgot he was carrying. He hoisted it over to Ágúst, thus fulfilling his duties as the *Intrepid* postman.

Many others of the colonists had already made their way to the tender to collect *Intrepid's* supplies he'd brought over and then load the supplies Ted was transporting back to the ship. Ted was only half paying attention, constantly looking for the one face he really wanted to see.

At this point the colonists flooded Ted with "hellos" and a drumbeat of questions about the *Intrepid* and its people; where they'd been, what they were doing, and so on. Ted was happy to answer whatever he could. This was their time to visit as well as his. It was never too long, especially if TJ wasn't there. Sometimes she was and other times she wasn't.

"Sorry, Ted," Ágúst said in his always measured tone. "She's out hunting today. She's up in the hills now. She thought you were coming yesterday."

Ted nodded. A while back, for their tender's protection, they decided not to broadcast the day of Ted's supply run. They were still afraid of pirates after a previous attack.

"I thought as much when I didn't see her."

"She's doing well. She really is."

"Don't touch me," hollered a high-pitched voice from the tender. "I get out on my own."

"So that's our newbie?" asked Jaga.

"Yep, Pasquale. Seems like a good kid. Lost his parents in the first attack. A few weeks ago, he failed the blood test. Then one day, he started screaming from his cabin and we saw that he was symptomatic. He was immediately placed in a cooler. He's struggled a lot since then. I've been praying with him, but he really needs some help from one of his own kind."

"You know we'll take care of him."

"I know you will. Say, how are you getting along with your parasitic neighbors?"

"That's something I wanted to talk to you about. I would recommend that you only come in the morning, while it's still cool. They hunt now and I'm afraid it's just not safe for you so late in the day."

"Got it. I'll get going then. Thanks." Ted shook his hand. "And please tell her hello from me. It's going to be hard to wait another month before I see her again."

"I will, Ted. Peace."

Ted waved to everyone and made his way back to the tender.

As he stepped into the water, he saw something sparkle, even though the sun was well shrouded today. He reached in and pulled up a familiar object: it was TJ's Orion necklace, the one he had given her and she said she had lost some four years ago. She must have lost it right here.

He turned back to the shore and gazed out toward the hills, where Ágúst said she was hunting. He didn't know why, probably just wishful thinking on his part, but he felt like she was watching him right then. He held the necklace up in the air, moving it so that its diamonds would reflect the dull sunlight from above. Then he placed it against his chest and crossed his arms: the sign language symbol for "love." Then he pointed to the hills. "You!"

He held his gaze for just a second longer before turning back to the tender.

TJ stood high upon a ridge, looking down upon her colony's beach. She crossed her arms over her chest and then pointed her finger at the tender a couple of miles away, her face glowing with joy.

"What are you doing, Mommy?" the little girl asked. She had one arm wrapped around TJ's knee and she gazed up with her ruby reds at the person who was the center of her young life.

TJ removed a foot from the deer she'd just killed and knelt down to pick up her daughter, marveling at how heavy a nearly four-year-old was.

"You see that man? The one now in that boat, with the gray beard and the blue cap, driving away?"

"Ah-hah," she said, not even having to squint to see him.

"That, my darling, is your daddy."

A Quick Word From The Author

Thank you for reading all the way to the end of this series. *MADNESS* has been an amazing journey for me, and I hope it has been for you as well.

In case you weren't aware, I'm an independent writer who relies on ratings and reviews to help get the word out about my books. This is why reviews are so important to me and why I truly need your help. Leaving even a short review would be greatly appreciated.

MLB

Post Review on Amazon

Is this really the end of MADNESS?

Even though over a year of research and planning went into the world of *MADNESS*, *MADNESS Chronicles* was intended to be a trilogy, and *Symptomatic* is the last installment of that trilogy. But that doesn't mean the *MADNESS* story is over.

In fact, if your feedback (through your reviews) makes it clear that I need to bring back the characters for more, I will. There are several follow up stories I have in mind, assuming the demand is there. Here are some of the many questions that remain unanswered...

What will become of the *Intrepid* and her crew?

What happens to Ted and/or TJ?

What about their daughter?

Can the island colony and neighboring parasitics coexist?

Will humans survive in this world?

Why do you want more?

Unleash your feedback (in your review): HERE

FREE BOOKS

Sign up for ML Banner's *Apocalyptic Updates* (VIP Readers list) and get a free copy of one of my best selling books:

In addition, you'll have access to our VIP Reader's Library, with at least four additional freebies.

Simply go here:

http://mlbanner.com/free
(and give me the email you want me to send your free book to)

Who is ML Banner?

Michael "ML" Banner is an award winning,
USA Today Bestselling author of Apocalyptic Thrillers

Michael writes what he loves to read: apocalyptic thrillers, which thrust regular people into extraordinary circumstances, where their actions may determine not only their own fate, but that of the world. His work is traditionally published and self-published.

Often his thrillers are set in far-flung places, as Michael uses his experiences from visiting other countries—some multiple times—over the years. The picture was from a transatlantic cruise that became the foreground of his award-winning *MADNESS Series*.

When not writing his next book, you might find Michael (and his wife) traveling abroad or reading a Kindle, with his toes in the water (name of his publishing company), of a beach on the Sea of Cortez (Mexico).

Want more from M.L. Banner?

MLBanner.com

Receive FREE books & *Apocalyptic Updates* - A monthly publication highlighting discounted books, cool science/discoveries, new releases, reviews, and more

Connect with M.L. Banner

Keep in contact – I would love to hear from you!
Email: michael@mlbanner.com
Facebook: facebook.com/authormlbanner
Twitter: @ml_banner

Books by M.L. Banner

For a complete list of Michael's current and upcoming books: MLBanner.com/new-projects/

ASHFALL APOCALYPSE

Ashfall Apocalypse (01)
A world-wide apocalypse has just begun.

Leticia's Soliloquy (An Ashfall Apocalypse Short)
(Exclusively available from a link at book #1 end)

Collapse (02)
As temps plummet, a new foe seeks revenge.

Compton's Epoch (An Ashfall Apocalypse Short)
Compton reveals what makes him tick.
(Exclusively available from a link at book #2 end)

Perdition (03)
Sometimes the best plan is to run. But where?

MADNESS CHRONICLES

MADNESS (01)
A parasitic infection causes mammals to attack.

PARASITIC (02)
The parasitic infection doesn't just affect animals.

SYMPTOMATIC (03)
When your loved one becomes symptomatic, what do you do?

The Final Outbreak (Books 1 - 3)
The end is coming. It's closer than you think. And it's real.

HIGHWAY SERIES

True Enemy (Short)
An unlikely hero finds his true enemy.
(USA Today Bestselling short only on mlbanner.com)

Highway (01)
A terrorist attack forces siblings onto a highway, and an impossible journey home.

Endurance (02)
Enduring what's next might cost them everything.

Resistance (03)
Coming Soon

STONE AGE SERIES

Stone Age (01)
The next big solar event separates family and friends, and begins a new Stone Age.

Desolation (02)
To survive the coming desolation will require new friendships.

Max's Epoch (Stone Age Short)
Max wasn't born a prepper, he was forged into one. (This short is exclusively available on MLBanner.com)

Hell's Requiem (03)
One man struggles to survive and find his way to a scientific sanctuary.

Time Slip (Stand Alone)
The time slip was his accident; can he use it to save the one he loves?

Cicada (04)
Cicada's scientific community... the world's only hope, or its end?

Made in the USA
Columbia, SC
21 June 2024

37322782R00150